George P. Rupp, College Girard

Semi-Centennial of Girard College

Biographical sketch of Stephen Girard, his will, and other papers relating to the

college and its development and government

George P. Rupp, College Girard

Semi-Centennial of Girard College
Biographical sketch of Stephen Girard, his will, and other papers relating to the college and its development and government

ISBN/EAN: 9783337096595

Printed in Europe, USA, Canada, Australia, Japan

Cover: Foto ©Andreas Hilbeck / pixelio.de

More available books at **www.hansebooks.com**

STEPHEN GIRARD
BY LAMBERT, FROM ORIGINAL BY OTIS. LIBRARY, GIRARD COLLEGE.

1848–1898.

———

SEMI-CENTENNIAL

OF

GIRARD COLLEGE.

BIOGRAPHICAL SKETCH OF STEPHEN GIRARD,
HIS WILL, AND OTHER PAPERS RELATING
TO THE COLLEGE AND ITS DEVELOP-
MENT AND GOVERNMENT.

ACCOUNT OF THE EXERCISES ON THE OCCASION
OF THE CELEBRATION OF THE OPENING
OF THE COLLEGE,

JANUARY 3, 1898.

———

PHILADELPHIA
GIRARD COLLEGE.
1898.

AT the request of the Committee in charge of the celebration this book is edited by

GEORGE P. RUPP.

Librarian.

GIRARD COLLEGE,
January, 1898.

PRESS OF
J. B. LIPPINCOTT COMPANY,
PHILADELPHIA.

CONTENTS.

3

LIST OF ILLUSTRATIONS.

1848-1898

Semi-Centennial Anniversary

GIRARD COLLEGE

PHILADELPHIA

JANUARY 3, 1898

Order of Exercises

MONDAY, JANUARY 3, 1898

2.30 P. M.

---

1. Selection—"Narcissus"   .   .   .   .   *Nevin*

2. Prayer
   ### WINTHROP D. SHELDON, A.M.
   Vice-President of Girard College

3. Introductory Remarks by the Chairman
   ### JOSEPH L. CAVEN, ESQ.
   Vice-President of the Board of Directors of City Trusts

4. Chorus— { a "Vesper Hymn"
            { b "The Happy Miller"

5. Address
   ### HON. CHARLES F. WARWICK
   Mayor of the City of Philadelphia

6. Waltz—"Abandoned"   .   .   *Waldteufel*

7. Address
   ### HON. MARRIOTT BROSIUS
   Member of Congress, Lancaster, Pa.

8. Hymn—"Hail Columbia"

9. Address
   ### THOMAS P. LONSDALE, '71
   President Girard College Alumni

10. Selection—"Genevieve de Brabant"   .   .   *Offenbach*

The Instrumental Music will be furnished by the
GIRARD COLLEGE BAND, GEORGE S. REYNOLDS, Leader
and the Vocal Music by the
PUPILS OF GIRARD COLLEGE, JERRY MARCH, Leader

Order of Exercises

MONDAY, JANUARY 3, 1898

8.00 P. M.

1. March—"The Stars and Stripes Forever"   .   .   *Sousa*

2. Prayer
   ### MR. B. B. COMEGYS
   Member of the Board of Directors of City Trusts

3. Introductory Remarks by the Chairman
   ### GEN. LOUIS WAGNER
   President of the Board of Directors of City Trusts

4. Caprice—"Hearts and Flowers"   .   .   *Tobani*

5. Historical Address
   ### ADAM H. FETTEROLF, LL.D.
   President of Girard College

6. Selection—"Popular Melodies"   .   .   .   *Beyer*

7. Address
   ### HON. THOMAS B. REED
   Speaker of House of Representatives, Washington, D. C.

8. Gems from the "Bohemian Girl"   .   .   .   *Balfe*

9. Address*
   ### HON. DANIEL H. HASTINGS
   Governor of the Commonwealth of Pennsylvania

10. Medley Overture—"National Airs"   .   .   .   *Coates*

11. Address
    ### THEODORE L. DeBOW, '57
    One of the First Hundred Boys admitted into the College

12. March—"El Capitan"   .   .   .   .   *Sousa*

The Music will be furnished by the
FIRST REGIMENT ORCHESTRA, S. H. KENDLE, Leader

---

*In the absence of Governor Hastings, Ethelbert D. Warfield, LL.D., President of Lafayette College, delivered an address.

Board of Directors of City Trusts

LOUIS WAGNER, President

JOSEPH L. CAVEN, Vice-President

ALEXANDER BIDDLE	JOHN K. CUMING
EDWARD S. BUCKLEY	WILLIAM L. ELKINS
JOHN M. CAMPBELL	JOHN H. MICHENER
BENJAMIN B. COMEGYS	DALLAS SANDERS
JOHN H. CONVERSE	EDWIN S. STUART

Members of the Board " Ex Officio"

CHARLES F. WARWICK, Mayor

JAMES L. MILES, Pres't Select Council

WENCEL HARTMAN, Pres't Common Council

FRANK M. HIGHLEY, Secretary   HON. F. CARROLL BREWSTER, Solicitor

Faculty of Girard College

ADAM H. FETTEROLF, Ph.D., LL.D., President

WINTHROP D. SHELDON, A.M., Vice-President

GEORGE J. BECKER	WARREN HOLDEN, A.M.
N. WILEY THOMAS, Ph.D.	JAMES N. WALKER, A.M.
FREDERICK PRIME, A.M., Ph.D.	JOHN K. HARLEY, M.E.
PIERRE FRANÇOIS GIROUD	CAPT. FRANK A. EDWARDS
Licencié ès Lettres (Univ. of France)	1st Cavalry, U. S. A.
CALIXTO GUITERAS, C.E.	ARCHIBALD COBB
C. ADDISON WILLIS, M.E.	MISS MARIAN B. HERITAGE

Librarian, GEORGE P. RUPP

Philadelphia, January 1, 1898

PREFATORY NOTE

Time tries all the thoughts and inventions of man.

In contemplating the progress of some great idea, time takes the place of perspective and plays the same part that distance does when we would comprehend the beauty and grandeur of a cathedral. Then we stand by the side of the architect, and see the building as he saw it in the secret chambers of his mind.

So the Semi-Centennial of Girard College afforded us similar conditions in the contemplation of the ideas of Stephen Girard. Different from other educational centres, his College is not merely a name, but it represents the real plan and belief of the Founder. Nowhere is there such an exhibition of one man's thought and work. The ideas of the Founder have been carried out by those administering them with an eye single to his wishes, and the best results have flowed from a rigid construction of his words.

That these results are potent fifty years after his death posterity may partly gather from this volume. Posterity will not, however, be able to comprehend the environments of the day celebrated, the great gathering of distinguished citizens, of graduates who had gone forth equipped for the battle of life, of pupils who are being trained for useful lives; the stately buildings and decorations, the brilliant illumination, and, finally, the air of festivity which no description can reproduce. But the addresses are here, and these will convey to the reader the thoughts of the orators.

If the Founder is conscious of what has been and is now being done in the fulfilment of his wishes, we may feel assured that he is satisfied with the efforts that are being made to care for and protect the orphan.

G. P. R.

GIRARD COLLEGE.   BUILDINGS NOS. 1 AND 2, LOOKING EAST.

FIFTIETH ANNIVERSARY OF THE OPENING OF GIRARD COLLEGE

January 1, 1848.   January 3, 1898.

BY FRANK M. HIGHLEY,

Secretary, Board of Directors of City Trusts.

At a stated meeting of the Board of Directors of City Trusts, held at their office, No. 120 South Third Street, Philadelphia, on Wednesday afternoon, June 9, 1897, the President called attention to the fact that on January 1, 1898, would occur the Semi-Centennial Anniversary of the Girard College for Orphans, it having been formally opened, with appropriate exercises, on January 1, 1848, and suggested that an event of so much importance should be celebrated in a manner commensurate with the world-wide renown of the College and its noble Founder.

Mr. Benjamin B. Comegys offered the following resolution, which was unanimously adopted:

"*Resolved*, That the Executive Committee be, and it is hereby, instructed to report a plan for the proper celebration of the Fiftieth Anniversary of the formal and official opening of Girard College on January 1, 1898."

The Chairmen of the several standing Committees, with the President of the Board, constitute the Executive Committee, as follows: Messrs. Louis Wagner, *President;* John H. Michener, Alexander Biddle, Benjamin B. Comegys, Joseph L. Caven, John H. Converse, Edward S. Buckley, and William L. Elkins.

13

The Committee, after fully considering the matter referred to them, submitted a plan for the celebration, which
was adopted by the Board. After a number of meetings,
the whole subject was referred to a special Sub-Committee,
consisting of Messrs. Wagner, Michener, Caven, and Converse.

The first day of January being a legal holiday and falling
on Saturday, it was agreed to celebrate the event on the
afternoon and evening of January 3.

The exercises were divided into two parts,—the one in
the afternoon to be for the officials and pupils of the College and the Alumni under twenty-one years of age, and
the evening meeting for the older Alumni and the invited
guests. Over five thousand invitations were sent to National, State and City officials, prominent educators, the
graduates of the College, and other distinguished citizens.

On the day of the celebration, the weather was most
propitious and beautiful.

The guests of the College were invited to thoroughly
inspect the Institution and to observe the liberal provisions made for the comfort and care of the pupils and
of the staff of the College. The grounds and buildings
were brilliantly illuminated by electric lights, and from the
central flag-staff the flag of the United States and the tri-
color of France spread their folds to the breeze.

The monument on the College grounds, erected in memory of the graduates who lost their lives in the suppression
of the Rebellion, was draped in the national colors. (The
bronze statue of Mr. Girard, on the City Hall Plaza, had
been adorned with a large laurel wreath and with streamers
of the College colors, and in the evening it was illuminated
by electric lights.) .

In the south vestibule of the Main Building the statue and sarcophagus of the Founder were enclosed in a miniature representation of the beautiful Main Building, which was handsomely illuminated by electric lights and profusely decorated with smilax and other plants and flowers, presenting a brilliant scene which was admired by everybody within the enclosure, as well as by the large crowds of people who gathered about the main entrance gates of the College, and were thus enabled to view it from a distance.

The afternoon and evening exercises were held in the Chapel, which was decorated with evergreens, plants, and bunting.

In front of the memorial window of President Allen, at the rear of the platform, hung a full length oil painting of Mr. Girard, which was kindly loaned by the Grand Lodge of Free and Accepted Masons of Pennsylvania; underneath gleamed in figures of light, the legend " 1848–1898."

The ceremonies of the celebration began promptly at 2.30 P.M., with Joseph L. Caven, Esq., Vice-President of the Board of Directors of City Trusts, as the presiding officer, and consisted of a prayer by W. D. Sheldon, A. M., Vice-President of the College; introductory remarks by the Chairman and addresses by Honorable Charles F. Warwick, Mayor of the City, Honorable Marriott Brosius, Member of the United States Congress, from Lancaster, Pennsylvania, Mr. Thomas P. Lonsdale, President of the Alumni of Girard College, and vocal and instrumental music by the pupils and the Band of the College.

During the performance of the musical selection which marked the close of the afternoon exercises, Honorable Thomas B. Reed, Speaker of the House of Representa-

tives, appeared upon the platform, escorted by General
Louis Wagner. The fifteen hundred pupils instantly rose
and greeted the distinguished visitor with cheers of wel-
come, and the applause was renewed when Chairman
Caven said:

" Boys, I present to you our honored guest."

Mr. Reed came forward and addressed the boys as
follows:

" Young gentlemen,—for all of you aspire to that title,
or I hope you will some day,—I am very much delighted
to see you; and I am going to make you much delighted
to see me by informing you that I am forbidden to make
a discourse. I content myself simply with wishing you
not only ' A Happy New Year,' but many of them."

The building was filled by a large and appreciative audience.

At the conclusion of the afternoon exercises, a reception
and dinner were given in Building No. 7 by the Board of
Directors of City Trusts to their distinguished guest, Honorable Thomas B. Reed, to which many prominent resi-
dents of the City and State were invited. This portion of
the celebration was under the direct charge and personal
supervision of Mr. John H. Michener, Chairman of the
Committee on Household, and, as was to be expected from
his broad experience, was complete in all its details, the
dining-room being a scene of rare beauty, with handsome
and elaborate decorations of electric lights, bunting, palms,
and plants; on the tables were placed large bunches of
American Beauty roses and other flowers. During the
reception and dinner, the music was furnished by a fine
orchestra.

Promptly at 8 P.M. Honorable Thomas B. Reed, the orator of the evening, escorted by the Board of Directors, and the invited guests entered the Chapel and occupied the platform.

An audience composed of graduates and distinguished citizens crowded the auditorium, the front seats being occupied by many of the Class of 1848.

General Louis Wagner, President of the Board of Directors of City Trusts, presided. The programme consisted of a prayer by Mr. Benjamin B. Comegys, a member of the Board of Directors; introductory remarks by the presiding officer; an historical address by A. H. Fetterolf, LL.D., President of the College, the oration by the Honorable Thomas B. Reed; and addresses by Ethelbert D. Warfield, LL.D., President of Lafayette College, and Mr. Theodore L. DeBow, one of the first one hundred boys admitted into the College, and instrumental music by the First Regiment Orchestra.

The several addresses were appropriate to the occasion, admirable in diction and eloquent in delivery, and all the exercises were greatly enjoyed by the enthusiastic audience, especially the peculiar mode in which the Chairman introduced the orator of the evening. He said:

"Mr. Reed, I have great pleasure in presenting to you these ladies and gentleman, citizens of Philadelphia, largely Alumni of Girard College, who have gathered to hear you talk to them on this important occasion."

This reversal of the usual form of introduction caused much amusement, and was received with great applause. A tumultuous greeting was given to Mr. Reed, and the audience listened to his address with close attention.

And thus ended a most fitting celebration of the opening of an Institution whose influence for good during the
fifty years of its existence is shown in the lives of the
nearly six thousand boys who have been admitted to its
care; and these, and other thousands yet to follow as pupils
in and graduates of Girard College, will tell during all time
of the boundless charity of its Founder.

GUESTS AT THE DINNER AND RECEPTION TENDERED HONORABLE THOMAS B. REED.

ADAMS, HON. ROBERT, JR.
ARNOLD, HON. MICHAEL
ASHMAN, HON. WILLIAM N.
AUDENREID, HON. CHARLES Y.
AUSTIN, WILLIAM L.
BEATH, COL. ROBERT B.
BECK, HON. JAMES M.
BEITLER, HON. ABRAHAM M.
BELL, JOHN C.
BIDDLE, COL. ALEXANDER
BINGHAM, HON. HENRY H.
BIRKINBINE, JOHN
BLAKELY, JOHN
BOYD, DR. JOHN S.
BREWSTER, FRANCIS E.
BROOKS, PROF. EDWARD
BROSIUS, HON. MARRIOTT
BUCKLEY, EDWARD S.
BURK, ADDISON B.
CAMPBELL, JOHN MARIE
CAVEN, JAMES
CAVEN, JOSEPH L.
CLOTHIER, CLARKSON
COGGESHALL, THELLWELL R.
COMEGYS, BENJAMIN B.
CONVERSE, JOHN H.
COOPER, HON. PETER L.
CROZER, SAMUEL A.
CUMING, JOHN K.
CUNNINGHAM, ERNEST
DeBow, THEODORE L.
DeGARMO, PROF. CHARLES
EDWARDS, CAPT. FRANK A.
ELKINS, WILLIAM L.
ELVERSON, JAMES

FELL, HON. D. NEWLIN
FERGUSON, HON. JOSEPH C.
FETTEROLF, ADAM H., LL.D.
FORST, DR. JOHN R.
GUITERAS, PROF. CALIXTO
HANNA, HON. WILLIAM B.
HARLEY, PROF. JOHN K.
HARRISON, CHARLES C., LL.D.
HARTMAN, WENCEL
HENSEL, GEORGE F.
HIGHLEY, FRANK M.
HOLDEN, PROF. WARREN
HOUSTON, PROF. EDWIN J.
JANNEY, DR. WILLIAM S.
JUNKIN, JOSEPH DE F.
KAERCHER, SAMUEL H.
KENDRICK, GEORGE W., JR.
KILPATRICK, WILLIAM H.
KIRKPATRICK, GEORGE E.
LAMBERT, MAJOR WILLIAM H.
LONSDALE, THOMAS P.
LUDWIG, PROF. DEB. K.
MacALISTER, PROF. JAMES
MacVEAGH, HON. WAYNE
McALEER, HON. WILLLAM
McLEAN, WILLIAM L.
McMICHAEL, HON. CHARLES B.
MICHENER, CHARLES G.
MICHENER, JOHN H.
MICHENER, J. HANSON, JR.
MILES, JAMES L.
MOORE, ALFRED
MORWITZ, JOSEPH
MUMFORD, JOSEPH P.
NEILSON, WILLIAM G.

PATTON, ALFRED G.
PAXSON, HON. EDWARD M.
PENNYPACKER, HON. SAMUEL W.
PERRINS, THOMAS
PESOLI, EDWARD A.
PRATT, CAPT. R. H.
PRIME, PROF. FREDERICK
QUICK, HARRY W.
REDNER, LEWIS H.
ROBINSON, THOMAS A.
RUPP, GEORGE P.
SANDERS, DALLAS
SCOTT, SAMUEL G.
SEARCH, THEODORE C.
SHARPLESS, ISAAC, LL.D.
SHELDON, PROF. WINTHROP D.
SHRIGLEY, JOHN M.
SMITH, HON. CHARLES EMORY
SNOWDEN, COL. A. LOUDON
SPARHAWK, JOHN, JR.

STONE, DR. JAMES F.
STUART, HON. EDWIN S.
THOMAS, PROF. N. WILEY
THOMPSON, MAJOR HEBER S
UNRATH, FREDERICK
VAUCLAIN, SAMUEL M.
WAGNER, MAJOR EMIL C.
WAGNER, GEN. LOUIS
WAGNER, LOUIS M.
WALKER, DR. J. B.
WALTON, CAPT. JOHN M.
WARFIELD, ETHELBERT D., LL.D.
WARWICK, HON. CHARLES F.
WATERALL, WILLIAM
WEED, PROF. GEORGE L.
WILLIAMS, HON. HENRY W.
WILLSON, HON. ROBERT N.
WILTBANK, HON. WILLIAM W.
WINDRIM, JAMES H.
WINDRIM, JOHN T.

ZESINGER, FRANK O.

EXERCISES—2.30 P.M.

GIRARD COLLEGE.   EAST PLAYGROUND.

PRAYER

BY WINTHROP D. SHELDON, A.M.,

Vice-President of Girard College.

Let us seek the Divine blessing.

Almighty and everlasting God and Father of all, we gather in Thy presence on this anniversary day with the voice of thanksgiving. We recall with gratitude and praise Thy favoring Providence, which has so richly blessed and prospered this school during all the years of its history. Thou didst breathe into the heart of its Founder those benevolent impulses and emotions, which prompted him to plan for it so thoughtfully and to endow it so generously. Thou hast bestowed wisdom and devotion upon those who from the beginning have been called to direct its affairs. And to the officers and teachers whom these passing years have united here in this labor of love, this blessed ministry to childhood and youth, Thou hast given faithfulness and zeal and the divine spirit of consecration. We bring Thee hearty thanks for the heritage of noble example and of faithful endeavor which those who have gone to their reward have left behind them here. And we beseech Thee, that in all the years to come there may be found those who shall be worthy to follow them, to carry forward this work and prosecute it to higher and yet more precious results. May the benediction of Heaven ever abide upon this Institution; upon those who administer its

23

affairs, that they may guard its interests wisely and with singleness of heart; upon the children and youth intrusted to its care, that they may receive such training as shall fit them to live soberly, righteously, and godly, in usefulness and service to their fellow-men; and upon its officers and instructors, that they may be endued with wisdom and grace from above, with the spirit of the Great Teacher, who came not to be ministered unto, but to minister. And to Thee shall be the praise now and evermore. Amen.

GIRARD COLLEGE. MAIN BUILDING.

INTRODUCTORY REMARKS

BY JOSEPH L. CAVEN, ESQ.,
Vice-President of the Board of Directors of City Trusts.

———————

PUPILS OF GIRARD COLLEGE:—In celebrating this Semi-Centennial Anniversary of your College, it is fitting you first should be gathered here; that you should be impressed as you never have been with the magnitude and munificence of this greatest of all bounties to the orphan boy.

Conceived in the mind and heart of Stephen Girard—childless and alone as he was—the seed he planted has become a great tree, the stream has become a great river, bearing hundreds into avenues of industry and prosperity that might otherwise have been wrecked in the passage of life.

Fifty years ago, the great plan mapped out by Mr. Girard was accomplished in the erection and completion of suitable buildings; 100 boys were then admitted, the roll of the College now numbers over 1500; its annual expense was then about $47,000, it is now $500,000.

The beautiful Main Building, after the design of a Greek temple, with its marble portico and thirty-four massive Corinthian columns, and four smaller buildings, two east and two west of the Main Building, then stood alone; now fourteen other buildings, constructed in harmony, stand on the grounds with those completed fifty years ago, all fully equipped, affording you a home, a training, and an education hard to excel.

This College has kept pace with the outside world. What is now the city of Philadelphia then had 500,000 inhabitants, now 1,200,000.

The State of Pennsylvania has grown from two and one-half millions to six millions of people; its mountains, valleys and plains are netted with railways; beneath its surface great mines of iron and coal have added to the material wealth of the great Commonwealth.

California was then admitted as a State of the Union. It was reached from the East by a long and dangerous ocean voyage, or a tedious trip with mule, horse and wagon over the plains; now we travel in a superbly appointed railroad train, and reach that great State in five days.

Canal-boats have given way to the railroad train, sailing vessels to the great steamships that cross the ocean in six days and a few hours. The news of the world is now read at our breakfast-table every morning. We sit in our office and comfortably and plainly converse with our friends one thousand or more miles away. Electricity has been tamed and controlled for our daily use as easily as the trainer controls the colt.

My boys, this is the brief record of your College, and the great world outside, during the past fifty years. What are its lessons to you at the beginning of the next fifty years? Will you in years to come be found among the worthy of this land, respected, honored, loved? Will you take a front rank in the world's industries and professions, adding to the already great store of new inventions and discoveries for the benefit of mankind? Or will you be a laggard in the ranks of the world's progress, leaving no impression and passing out of mind unregretted?

The great past has been hewed and carved out by such as you—can the future depend on you for greater developments?

This celebration is now opened, and if, when over, your heads, your hearts and your minds respond, "For the years to come we will do our best," these exercises shall not have been in vain.

ADDRESS

BY HON. CHARLES F. WARWICK,

Mayor of the City of Philadelphia.

MR. CHAIRMAN, LADIES AND GENTLEMEN, BOYS OF
GIRARD COLLEGE:—Owing to the pressure of business engagements it has been impossible for me to find time in
which to prepare a set address, and, while hurrying to this
anniversary meeting and thinking what I should say to
you, I came suddenly into these grounds, and before
me stood a magnificent structure. I refer to your Main
Building, which is known the wide world over as Girard
College. It gave me a text. This is said to be the finest
specimen of the Corinthian order of architecture of modern
times; and perhaps very few structures of the past, even
in the golden days of Greece, when the Doric, the Ionic
and the Corinthian orders were conceived and assumed
shape and form, ever surpassed in beauty of proportion,
in delicacy of outline, or in perfection of symmetry, the
building to which I refer. It is an adornment not only to
the city, but also stands for one of the greatest benefactions of modern times; and when we bear in mind that
this great Institution sprang from the benevolence, the
humanity, the love of a single heart, we may begin to appreciate the purpose of Mr. Girard's life and the charity
of his soul.

Who can measure, even approximately, the influence of

28

STEPHEN GIRARD.
STATUE AND SARCOPHAGUS, MAIN BUILDING, GIRARD COLLEGE.

this great Institution, an influence that is circumscribed by time alone; for it will go on distributing its blessings through untold ages yet to come, sending out into the world an army, we may say armies, of boys fully equipped for the battle of life, physically, morally and intellectually trained, and with every opportunity, in this free country of ours, to become useful citizens and to make for themselves reputation and to win fame.

Let it be borne in mind, too, that these advantages are for those who, in the vast majority of instances, without the care of this Institution would lack the favor and the blessings of education.

How deeply grateful you should be to the Founder of this College! You truly may call him father, for you are his children. Most bountifully he has provided for you out of his store, and you will be faithless and ungrateful if you do not honor him, by making a suitable return in earnest and honest lives. In this connection, let me further say that it is your duty to patriotically serve that city which has so safely guarded this trust and which provides for you so great an opportunity. I think it may be said without the fear of contradiction that no public trust has ever been more successfully and more honorably administered with an eye single to the interests of all concerned.

You are all familiar with the life of Stephen Girard, and I am not able to add a single incident not already known. It is a simple story, quickly told, but in some particulars it is heroic in character. He was not commonplace, as some would have you believe, but was characterized by industry, by earnestness of purpose, by exceptional business foresight and ability, by humanity, and by a courage that arose at times to the dignity of heroism.

He was born away back in the middle of the last century in Bordeaux, France. We know comparatively but little of his early years; if some accounts be true, his home life was not the happiest. He did not enjoy any special advantages in the matter of his early education; he had to make his own career and attain his own success; but he possessed those qualities or traits that tend to make a man not only successful but useful.

The town in which he was born was a busy, trading seaport, and he early turned his attention to maritime pursuits. It was an undertaking of no little importance in those days to cross the ocean. The pathway of the Atlantic was not then crowded, as it is to-day, with fast-flying steamers. A sailing-vessel then took six weeks, and sometimes longer, to make a voyage from the old world to the new; the average time now of first-class steamers is about six days. Travel is a great educator for attentive minds, and we can easily understand how a seafaring life broadened the views of Mr. Girard, for he was always a keen, close observer, and ever took his lessons from the busy, practical side of life. He was essentially a man of affairs. The new world had special attractions for a man of Mr. Girard's energy and industry. It opened up to him a new field and afforded him opportunities that the old world could never have given.

It was a fortunate day for us when Providence directed his steps to this city and he decided to make Philadelphia his permanent home. His business success was marvellous,—his every venture met with favor, his ships sailed every ocean and touched at every port. From Philadelphia to London, from London to Calcutta, his vessels were ploughing the seas, uniting the different nations in the bonds of commerce and international trade. He was the leading merchant of this country, and made this city the commercial centre of the new world; and you must bear in mind that when he began his business career here, he was a stranger in a strange land, and had to overcome those obstacles that would not have been in the way of one "to the manor born." He had to acquire a new tongue, make new friends, and live down prejudice and envy. He had a genius for business; his judgment was good, or what might be called safe; he intuitively knew the market, its conditions and its necessities. He lived plainly, economically, but comfortably; he devoted himself so assiduously to business that he had no time nor desire for so-called social "functions." He was never given to ostentation. He gave no sumptuous banquets, but he was laying up a store that was to feed and clothe the humble and the homeless.

Did you ever bear this fact in mind, that it was for you he labored, it was for you he accumulated his fortune, it was for you he devoted the energies of his life? I speak thus plainly, because I want to bring home to you these facts in simple form, that on this anniversary day I may arouse in your hearts love for him who did so much for you.

I have already said that he at times rose to the dignity of heroism. Not only was he a man of charity but also of courage. If there is anything in the world that shows the real quality of a man, it is when he faces an impending danger for the sake of humanity from which others turn and flee. In time of great public calamity or peril, when courage wavers and the bravest hearts quail, he who goes into the breach and meets the danger with fortitude is a master among men. No man is mean of heart who has courage of soul.

We come now to an incident in Mr. Girard's life which reveals to us the real character of the man, and we should judge men by what they do, rather than by what others say of them.

In the year 1793 this city was visited by a plague, a pest known as yellow fever; it was unusually deadly in its touch and the population became panic-stricken. Those who were able to leave their homes, fled. Every house was under the shadow of death. The ambulances rumbled through the city by night and by day, and the dead carts hurried their victims to speedy burial. Affection waned and humanity lost its gentleness; parents left their children to die, and children abandoned their parents. The merciless pest carried fear and desolation in every direction,— houses were closed, business was suspended, grass grew in the streets, and the churches were turned into hospitals.

At this time Mr. Girard was in the very vigor and prime of manhood, on the very flood-tide of his business success, the richest man in the city. He could easily have fled, could have taken refuge elsewhere, and could have waited until the danger passed away, but he refused to turn his back upon his stricken, suffering fellow-men. He listened to the call for help and opened his heart and his purse, and not only this, but volunteered to serve as a nurse, and for two months was in attendance upon the sick and the dying in a public pest-house.

Take this incident in his life, and then bear in mind his benefaction, and can any one doubt his great humanity? Willing in public peril to risk his life for his fellow-man, he subsequently gave the labor of his years to the creation of

one of the sweetest charities of modern times. Courage
and charity! Where is there a life in which there have
been shown greater qualities of heart and soul than in that
of this man, so little understood and appreciated in his day
and generation?

Oh, how little we know of the real sentiments and qualities of men while they live, and while envy and detraction
unite with "small talk" and slander to blast, to blemish
and destroy! Pity 'tis, we cannot in some way make
amends, for the indifference that was shown him in his
day by many of his fellow-citizens, who followed him with
scandal even to the grave. Childless and surrounded by
strangers he passed away, but to a reward, we hope,
greater than man can give. Though maligned in life and
misunderstood, his humanity was not fathomed until his
spirit sank to rest. When his will was opened, he was
found to be the greatest philanthropist this country, up to
that time, had ever known. His charity was so broad and
so far reaching, that it linked him with the infinite, with
that just God who is the searcher of all hearts, and who
is able to find the truth, no matter how deep it may be
buried, or how far from the sight of man it may be hidden.

You may tell me that such a man had no creed, but you
cannot urge that he was without faith. He wore no broad
phylacteries, he indulged in no cant, he mouthed not his
prayers in public places, but his heroism and his charity
show such magnanimity of soul, that his love for man but
reflects his love for God. He expressed his faith in noble
works. His charity will go out to future generations to
bless, to comfort, and to save, increasing in its usefulness
as the years multiply, and, as we look out into the future,
little can we measure the extent and greatness of his

bounty. He turned not back from his duty; he faced death when others quailed, and he bequeathed his fortune to those whom he did not know, but whom he sincerely loved.

This Institution is a monument to his charity, to his humanity, to his magnanimity, and it speaks more eloquently in his favor than could a thousand tongues in pompous eulogy. This Institution is the tender response of his heart to the appeal from the fatherless for help and comfort.

Philadelphians are beginning to understand the real qualities of Mr. Girard; they are becoming more familiar with the man, and more keenly appreciative of the extent of his great bounty. They know the usefulness of the College, but they have had a misconception of the real motives of the donor and the qualities that characterized him.

After his death, the long litigation over his will, the stories that were set in circulation by his enemies, the statement that he had no religious faith, all tended to blind the judgment and to darken the truth, but now, weighing his deeds, we are better able to judge him and to know him in his true light.

His life is interwoven into the history of our city; his charity has come to bless us, and, as time runs on, his memory will be more and more honored and revered. Truly it can be said of him that

> " He had a tear for pity and a hand
> Open as day for melting charity."

This is but a sketch of his life briefly told, but compare his career, if you will, with that of other great characters in history. I read the other day in a newspaper, that Bismarck had expressed his regret for having provoked quarrels that resulted in bloodshed. The statement may or may not have been true, but it has its lesson.

I wonder if Napoleon, in his rock-bound prison far out in the ocean, ever looked back upon his past and realized the misery that had been wrought by his ambition; how cruel had been his wars, how selfish and wicked had been his purposes, how he had set at defiance every moral obligation and every precept of God and man. The remains of this great soldier lie to-day in a beautiful and imposing tomb in the Hôtel des Invalides, and his memory is honored by his countrymen.

Contrast the life of Napoleon in usefulness with that of this quiet citizen and man of peace, who brought fortune and fame to our city, whose history is not written in blood, but in charity, who watched over the sick and held the cup to the parched lips of the dying, who gave to us one of the greatest bounties ever bequeathed by a citizen of America for the benefit of humanity. Bear all this in mind, and ever hold in grateful remembrance the name and kindness of your benefactor; then this Semi-Centennial Anniversary will not have been held in vain.

MAN AND CITIZEN.—AN ADDRESS

BY HON. MARRIOTT BROSIUS,

Member of Congress, Lancaster, Pennsylvania.

"And, especially, I desire that, by every proper means, a pure attachment to our republican institutions and to the sacred rights of conscience, as guaranteed by our happy Constitution, shall be formed and fostered in the minds of the scholars."—*Will of Stephen Girard.*

I will not conceal the satisfaction it gives me to unite with the faculty, alumni and students of this Institution in commemorating the Semi-Centennial Anniversary of its founding; and I tender them my cordial felicitations on this auspicious celebration of a "golden wedding." Fifty years ago, at this place, Opulence and Opportunity were united in the bonds of a wedlock whose numerous progeny of blessings to the human family afford convincing proof that the children have obeyed the Divine injunction, have honored their father and their mother, and their days will be long in the land. That the splendid success of the Institution has been largely due to the wisdom of its management goes without saying; yet, the noble example of its illustrious Founder, the "mariner and merchant," "humanitarian and philanthropist," "noble man and public-spirited citizen," which has been speaking all these years to the youth who have enjoyed the advantages of his munificent gift to noble uses, must have had a commensurate agency in achieving such magnificent results.

36

In his last will and testament, Stephen Girard laid his command upon all who should touch these foundations or lay their hands to the upbuilding of this temple dedicated to the care, comfort, and culture of orphaned boys. He expressed his desire that, by every proper means, a pure attachment to our republican institutions and to the sacred rights of conscience, as guaranteed by our happy Constitution, should be formed and fostered in the minds of the scholars.

Obedience to this testamentary injunction will secure two results of the first importance to human society. It will form good men and make good citizens. An object so worthy of our pursuit at all times as the betterment of man in his relations to society and the state may well engage our special attention on this commemorative occasion.

It was the thought of Lowell that the first duty of the United States is to become a nation of men builders; but, when we contemplate the mixed quality of human nature, how good and evil are blended, how the serpent's hiss and the bird's song are mingled in its composition, we realize how arduous is the task.

When Leonardo da Vinci was painting his famous fresco, "The Last Supper," on the wall of a Dominican convent, the prior became impatient at the tardiness of the work and reproached the painter, who, answering, said, " I still want two faces, one of which, the Saviour, I cannot hope to find on earth, and I have not attained the power of presenting it to myself in imagination with all the perfection of beauty and spiritual grace demanded in a representation of the Divine Incarnation; the other is that of Judas, and I hardly think it possible to render graphically

3

the features of a man who, after receiving so many benefits from Him, deliberately betrayed his Lord and Master."

Similarly, he who undertakes to depict in words the
extremes of goodness and badness in human character,
like Leonardo, will be unable to complete his pictures, for
no mastery of the art of characterization will enable him
adequately to portray the radiant image of the divine in
man at his best, or to graphically render the dark incarnation of evil in him at his worst.

"Compound of beast and angel, of devil and deity,"
said Coleridge. "The glory and the scorn of the uni-
verse," said Pascal. "A jewel of God," said Parker. "A
rapacious vulture," said Cowley. "Half dust and half
deity; alike unfit to sink or soar," said Byron. What an
inharmonious being! How noble in reason, yet how
prone to error; how infinite in faculty, yet how low in desire; in form and moving how express and admirable, yet
how low he bends to vice and folly; in action how like an
angel, in acts how like a devil; in apprehension how like
a god, yet in appetite how like a brute! This is man in
his totality; but, as Emerson suggests, man has been dif-
ferentiated into men, good men, middling men, and bad
men; so we can conceive them in their several characters
and distinguish one from the other.

It is man at his best, God's noblest work except woman,
that I want my words this afternoon to help you to build.
Michael Angelo, walking in the streets of Florence, saw
a block of marble in some rubbish at his feet. He stooped
to pick up the stone. His friend asked him what he
wanted with the worthless rock. Angelo replied, with the
enthusiasm that only genius feels, "There is an angel in
that stone, and I must get it out." He took it to his

studio, and, by patient toil with mallet and chisel, he let
the angel out. So, in every orphan boy who enters this
College, there is the rough marble of a magnificent manhood. Wise, indeed, is this management if, with the
hammer and chisel of precept, example and instruction,
it carves the marble of the soul into the beauty of Christian
manhood.

This is the work in which Girard College is engaged.
Its Founder meant that it should stand for the highest
conceivable things, for manhood, for character, for conscience, for courage, for those higher things which are
raising the walls of the great temple of character, a temple
whose altar is the eternal right, whose high priest is conscience, whose ritual is duty, whose prayer is service,
whose song is love.

In the culture of character, soul tillage, or the building
of a man, the things of first importance are the principles
of right conduct which give character to the man. Dwell
with me briefly on some of these first principles.

No character can approach perfection without what
Charles Lamb called "incorrigible and immovable honesty." This is the backbone of an erect and sovereign
soul. Nor is it a difficult achievement. It only requires
the subjection of our daily conduct to the direction of the
law of our spiritual life. This trait fixed, you command
every man's respect. Your neighbor is your witness. He
feels safe in your company, for he knows you will be
honest in the dark and virtuous without a witness. He
believes a portion of divinity is incarnated in you, and
whither you go, here or hereafter, others will be pleased to
have your company, for they know, without consulting
their catechism, that the soul of an honest man will lend a

charm to the everlasting rest of the saints. The late lamented Father Taylor, a devout Methodist, in an observation quite worth remembering, has emphasized the value of integrity of soul as a passport to the blessings hoped for. His brethren were criticising his friendship for Emerson, and insisting that the philosopher, being a Unitarian, must go to the place some people think it not polite to mention. "It does look so," said Father Taylor; " but I am sure of one thing: if Emerson goes to that place, he will change the climate there and emigration will set that way."

Honesty means a steadfast adherence to our principles, which is a very arduous task for some people who, from the unsteadiness of their conduct, seem to be destitute of both chart and compass. They illustrate the idea Lowell put in the mouth of one of his characters:

> " A marciful Providence fashioned us holler
> On purpose that we might our principles swaller."

No man can honor his principles if he is ashamed of them; he can only be true to them when he glories in them. I heard of a minister who preached a sermon against intemperance, and, finding that a liquor dealer was present, went to him and apologized for criticising his business. The minister learned a lesson in honesty from the reply of the liquor dealer. He said, " Oh, never mind; that's all right. You would have to preach an all-fired poor sermon if you didn't hit me somewhere."

The National Assembly of France, a century ago, set at least one glittering star on its forehead which has been shining with fadeless lustre down the years. When it was discovered that Mirabeau had been guilty of dishonesty, it caused his body to be removed from the Pantheon and interred among criminals, because the Assembly decreed that none but the remains of great men could lie in the French Pantheon, and no man could be great without honesty.

My young friends, I charge you, remember there are but two sides,—"God's truth and the Devil's falsehood." Rise to the former and you are an upright, heaven-facing creature; you are a man. No eye can shame you. Conscious rectitude gives you self-respect and the respect of others. Truth is a part of the machinery of God, and, when you put yourselves in gear with that machinery, you have the Almighty to turn your wheels. But fall to the latter, and you stand before your neighbor with a shamed face, before your own soul with a downcast eye, before God with a sense of degrading guilt, and you are less than a man.

The man I am outlining is a moral hero. There is, perhaps, no other quality in which the average man is so deficient as heroism. How many of us lack the courage of our convictions! Celestial professions and terrestrial practices go hand in hand. Many render lip homage to the principles of right living whose hearts are lightly touched with devotion to their claims. If the bronze lips of Philadelphia's patron saint would break into speech and tell to all the inhabitants of the city the incident Gladstone tells of Lord Melbourne, fifty thousand men would recognize their own likeness. Melbourne was seen coming from church one Sabbath in great excitement. Meeting a friend, he exclaimed, "It is too bad. I have always been a supporter of the church and have always upheld the clergy; and it is really too bad to have to listen to a sermon like that I heard this morning. Why, the preacher actually insisted upon applying religion to a man's private life."

How many fail for lack of heroism to meet and conquer adverse fate! I have read that, in an art gallery in Antwerp some years ago, one could have seen a celebrated painter copying from the great masters. He was born without arms, but with an ambition kindled with the love of art. By patient toil, he trained his feet to perform the functions of hands, until he could mix his colors, and deftly upon the canvas reproduce the best works of the old masters. He was a hero.

In society, conformity is the line of least resistance. The average man is a moral chameleon and takes the prevailing hue. He would like to set a better fashion, but he lacks the courage. His moral standard is as high as that of the presidential candidate who said he would like to have the Lord on his side, but he must have the State of Kentucky. The man who possesses the heroism of sterling manhood, the sublimity of devotion to high ideals, finds his battle-field wherever he finds a foe to right, a cause that needs assistance, or a wrong that lacks resistance. He never stops to count the number of his adversaries when truth is assailed, and he never capitulates to circumstances, badges, fashions, or institutions; but, in the midst of the crowd, he keeps his independence and holds his rudder true.

When Raphael was drawing his figures too small, Michael Angelo sketched a colossal head before his eyes and taught him his fault. It is the duty of the moral hero to sketch the figures of right conduct in their true proportion and lift high the level of the fashion.

The world enjoys a perpetual dowry in the memory of her heroes, and the living catch heroic fire from the contemplation of the heroism that proclaimed its principles amid flames, that showed its faith under the axe, that went with Shadrach to the fiery furnace and with Daniel to the lion's den.

The other day I opened a volume of Mazzini's "Essays" and read how, upon a day in the sixteenth century at Rome, inquisitors were assembled to compel a prisoner to renounce the truth he had declared. The prisoner was Galileo. His soul revolted against the violence of those who sought to force him to deny what he knew was an eternal verity. His strength was exhausted by suffering; the monkish menace had crushed him. He raised his hand to declare a lie, but at the same time he raised his weary eyes to heaven and caught a ray from the eternal which kindled his conscience, and the great truth again burst from the believer's soul in those memorable words: "Epur se muove" ("It moves nevertheless"). That sublime cry of Galileo still floats above the ages, teaching the children of men that heroism is the highest outlook of the soul.

Daniel O'Connell, in the House of Commons, offered twenty-seven votes for every Irish measure if he would not ally himself with the anti-slavery party, spurning the splendid bribe and declaring, "Gentlemen, God knows I speak for the saddest people the sun sees, but may my right hand forget its cunning and my tongue cleave to the roof of my mouth if, to save Ireland, I forget the slave of any land," was a hero of unrivalled splendor. Garrison, in the face of the world's contempt, declaring, "I will be as harsh as truth, as uncompromising as justice; I will not equivocate, I will not excuse, I will speak out, I will be heard," was a hero. Abraham Lincoln, in the midst of collisions of opinion and the distractions of war, declaring, " Whatever seems to be God's will I will do," was a hero. General Grant, with the vanquished army of the rebellion at his feet, saying, " Lay down your arms; go to your homes on your parole of honor, and take your horses with you to cultivate your farms, but come and take dinner with us before you go," was a hero. Our souls should bow in reverence before the temple which enshrines these divinities of heroism.

But our man—the Girard College brand—is not yet complete. He must be benevolent. The founder of this Institution, by his splendid munificence, has given this noble trait distinct pre-eminence; and it is a happiness to know that his illustrious example has had many imitators. No other country has so many millionaires as our own, and in no other have rich men used their wealth in such beneficent ways. It is estimated that the money given for benevolent uses by wealthy Americans through institutions whose benefits are shared by the people, counting no gifts under $5,000, averages $30,000,000 a year. This shows that the trend of development in man is toward a higher plane of life. Philosophers say, if evolution throws any light upon existence, it shows that man is a spiritual being, and that the direction of his long career is toward more exalted living, and that one day the human race will flower into perfect beings who will live by the Golden Rule. John Fiske insists that the development of the higher spiritual qualities of man is the goal toward which nature's work has tended from the beginning. Victor Hugo believed, with some complacency, that he was the tadpole of an archangel. Huxley says if it is not so, if there is no hope of a large improvement in the human family, he would hail the advent of some kindly comet to sweep it all away. But it is so, and the incontestable evidence of it is found in the number of munificent gifts for the benefit of the human family which have conferred honorable distinction upon Americans of opulence, and of which the splendid gift of Stephen Girard will ever remain a conspicuous example. It illustrates how, in the ascent of man, he passes from the plane of the struggle for life, to that of the struggle for the lives of others; from what Henry Drummond calls self-regarding to other-regarding conduct, which is, distinctly, a higher plane. It means that we are more and more recognizing our brother as in our keeping, and are learning to value the things of this world for their service to mankind, and more and more to regard wealth as a trust, to be employed in wise and beneficent uses, for the benefit of our fellow-men. And thus the principle of benevolence becomes a necessary element in every well-formed character; and I would have you cherish it as one of the ties which hold the human family in the bonds of unity and peace; for we must never forget "that we are children of the same Father, travelling toward the same home, and hoping to sit down at last at the same banquet, and, therefore, we should love and help one another."

But our man has not yet reached his full stature. He must be sensible of the obligations of duty. Society is organized on the basis of the performance of duty. Indifference, or neglect here, not only puts a blemish on character, but tends to the disintegration of social order. Let me drive this thought home with a passage from

"Christmas Carol," whose pathos and power affect me more than the profoundest utterances of philosophy on the necessity of fidelity to the duties our social relations impose. When Scrooge ventured the conciliatory suggestion that Marley was a good man of business, the ghost replied, "Business! Mankind was my business; the common welfare was my business; charity, mercy, forbearance and benevolence were all my business. The dealings of my trade were but a drop of water in the comprehensive ocean of my business." The moral so sharply pointed by this persuasive message to the living, from a spirit in chains of its own forging while in life is, that no devotion to mere personal ends, can absolve us from the larger obligations we owe society.

When Stephen Girard took his life in his hands, and entered the loathsome pest-house at Bush Hill, to nurse the sick and comfort the dying, he set a shining example of devotion to duty and exemplified the thought of the poet:

"'Tis man's perdition to be safe
When for man he ought to die."

Young people are beset with temptations to neglect their duty. It may be the siren voice of pleasure or pride, indifference or indolence, that lures them from their post or lulls them to sleep. Every time they yield to the solicitations of the tempter they lose a portion of their power of resistance, and victory is harder at the next assault. The young man who believes that he can win the crown of noble manhood, without bearing the cross of duty, or achieve the glory of victory, without the sweat and dust of the race, suggests Saul with a difference. The latter went out to find his father's asses and came back to find himself a king; but the former goes out a king, in his **own** conceit, and comes back to find himself the other **animal.**

In the museum of the Stanford University in California I saw an **impressive painting** illustrating "duty." **I was** reminded how apt men are in asserting their rights, and how inapt they are in assuming their duties. A central figure represents Law; another, Justice. On the left, a youth holds a scroll, on which is written, "Rights of Man." An aged priest near by reminds the youth that man has a heritage of duty as well as rights. In the fore-ground, two children are reading a scroll bearing the in-scription, "No Rights without Duties." It is a lesson for the ages.

Young man, let **duty be a part of your religion.** You can follow the example of the shipmaster in the story. He prayed to Neptune, "O God, Thou canst save me if Thou wilt, or destroy me; but, however it be, I will keep my rudder true."

The question of every soul, "What shall I do to **gain** eternal life?" is nowhere more clearly answered than in Schiller's noble **lines:**

> "Thy duty ever,
> Discharge aright the simple duties with
> Which each day is rife ; yea, with thy might."

Now, my friends, we have considered the most essential parts of the structure of a man; let us now crown him with the **noble mind's** distinguishing perfection,—honor This is the **graceful ornament of man,** the Corinthian capi-tal of the stately **column of Christian manhood.** It is so nearly allied to **honesty, I** need not dwell upon it. **Yet** there is a distinction, **subtle, perhaps,** but appreciable. It is **the finest essence, the** distilled spirit, the soul of honesty. The true man feels the obligations of honor superior to all others. In every rank and condition of life, in every vocation, it is a sure passport to veneration and affection. A tradesman once asked Charles James Fox to pay him a debt from some money he was counting. Fox replied, " I owe this money to another: it is a debt of honor; he has nothing to show for it." " Then," said the tradesman, " I change my claim to a debt of honor," and he tore the note to pieces. Fox thanked his creditor for his confidence and paid him the money, saying, " The other man must wait; yours is the oldest debt."

When Washington applied to Robert Morris for a large sum of money for the use of the army, the latter went, despondent, to the street in search of funds. He met a wealthy Quaker, to whom he made his wants known. " Robert, what security canst thou give?" asked the Friend. " My note and my honor," Morris replied. " Thou shalt have it" was the Quaker's prompt response.

These instances have the flavor of the millennium, and are a foretaste of the happy condition of society when engagements are all kept, and, hence, always accepted; when all men are like Stephen Girard, whose word was as good as his bond, and honor is man's distinguishing perfection.

Now, we have our man; we have made him, not in our own image, but in the likeness of an ideal that is attainable. We have not made him a Calvinist, but we have made sure of his orthodoxy in the five essential points of the moral code of noble manhood. It was Stephen Girard's first concern that the purest principles of morality should be instilled in the mind of youth, and it was no part of our purpose to exceed these bounds.

But the man is to be a citizen, and that calls into requisition another element of character which brings him into relations with his country. The proudest title the ancient Roman knew was " Civis sum Romanus," " I am a Roman citizen." A nobler and prouder title is ours: " Civis sum Americanus," " I am an American citizen." As no other decoration ever rivalled this in splendor and no other title ever carried so many rights, privileges and honors; so it must be said, and with a solemn sense of its deep import, no other relation lays on us such commanding duties or imposes such responsible obligations to our country.

Patriotism means a due sense of these obligations and duties, with a commensurate disposition to their observance and performance. It is not a mere ephemeral passion; it is an enduring emotion, an eternal ray that kindles the soul into the glory of service and sacrifice for country. It constrains to good citizenship.

It concerns us now to know what is meant by a " good citizen." And this inquiry derives importance from a distinguishing feature of our system, sometimes called the " hydrostatic paradox" of popular government. In a bent tube, with one arm a foot in diameter and the other no larger than a pipe-stem, the water will stand the same height in both. Similarly, universal suffrage equalizes the votes of the philosopher and the fool, the President and the pauper. It is easily seen that under such a system —and it may be the best for us—the active virtues of the citizen are not only the breath of our present life, but of our life to come as a nation.

Now, I will tell you what constitutes a good citizen. That I have told it elsewhere will not diminish its truth. A citizen who is a sovereign must be qualified for his kingdom; he must be moulded on forms of virtue, self-restraint, obedience and loyalty to conscience and country; he must be self-governing in the wide range of activities which lie outside the sanction of the statute and far away from the policeman's beat; he must have fineness and strength in the warp of intelligence, and firmness of texture in the woof of virtue; he must subject his political conduct to the restraints of moral principle, and subordinate his private interests to his public duties; he must not yield to the delusive plausibilities of untutored demagogues; he must not be content with holding right opinions, but must strive to make them prevalent; he must not be lulled to repose by the delusion that he does no harm who takes no part in public affairs; he must know that the apathy of the patriot is the opportunity of the knave; he must not bend the knee to boss or Baal, nor refuse the guidance of superior wisdom and recognized statesmanship; he must never find it his interest to be ignorant of what it is his duty to know; he must never treat the public purse with less consideration than his neighbor's pocket; he must never sleep on his post or desert to the enemy; he must never cease to improve himself, but must never call in the enemies of his principles to correct his defects.

That is the man I have fashioned in your hearing, in the character of a citizen, and you can plainly see I gave him no endowment that he can spare from his equipment for this exalted rôle. You may say this is an ideal citizen, fit only for the republic of Plato, or the Utopia of Sir Thomas More; but patriotism can transmute the ideal into the real citizen, and it must do so if our institutions are to endure. That is the meaning of Stephen Girard's injunction, that a pure attachment to our republican institutions should be formed and fostered in the minds of the scholars. Our form of government contemplates .such citizens, and only such can be effective in working out the purpose of all our political machinery, to give ascendancy to the forces fittest to govern and to bring the best reason and conscience to expression in the government of the state.

These desirable results require the best men to take a part in the agencies which form and guide the collective action. The good citizen should do his own thinking. He should climb to the best outlook and come to his own conclusions. He should strive to be a man of light and leading in his community. He must distinguish the counterfeit from the real sentiment of the people; he must not be misled by the cry swelled by the least capable. The noisy few ofttimes arrest more attention than the quiet multitude. He must avoid "foolometers," which Sydney Smith defines as "the acquaintance of a few regular fools as a test of public opinion," and, which I regret to say, is too much in vogue in our public life. He must avoid the dangerous delusion suggested by John Fiske, that civil government in the United States dropped from heaven, or was specially created by miracle, and will continue to run by divine agency, without the aid of the citizen,—in other words, that Providence takes care of children, idiots and the United States. It has been truly said that God has never endowed any statesman or philosopher with wisdom enough to frame a system of government that everybody could go off and leave. Some people in politics are like the philosopher who, when informed that his house was on fire, coolly replied, "Go tell my wife; I never meddle with household affairs."

And so the outposts of good government are abandoned, the patriot army furloughed, government falls into disrepute, the State suffers, the city languishes for a breath of pure political air, the public service is inefficient because plundered by profligate politics, the honor of the government is tarnished, its power enfeebled, its administration corrupted, its glory dimmed, because a portion of the people who have no motive to make other than the best possible government abstain from participation in political duties. This is not patriotism or good citizenship. It is culpable neglect, if not base cowardice.

I commend to you nobler examples of citizenship and grander ideas of duty. General Sherman said, "Teach your children to honor the flag, to respect the laws, and to love and understand our institutions, and our glorious country will be safe." General Meade, taking his farewell of the Army of the Potomac, said, "Let us earnestly pray for strength and light to discharge our duties as citizens."

Now, my young friends, I have shown you a man and a citizen. I have brought to your view the principles whose cultivation the Founder of this College enjoined, for he knew they were indispensable to good men and good citizens. I have coupled them with examples for your study. If you value the principles, you will emulate the examples and make your lives worthy the inheritance of blessings you enjoy, and show the world the bright and perfect flower of Christian manhood and American citizenship.

/

ADDRESS

BY THOMAS P. LONSDALE, '71,

President of the Girard College Alumni.

———————

In the reflected light of the noble sentiments so eloquently expressed by the distinguished speakers who have
preceded me, some ray, I trust, may illuminate my humble
tribute to this memorable occasion.

Leaving the College in 1871, the midway point almost of
the period we celebrate to-day, the men and interests that
filled those fateful years of the first half are a vanishing
memory, peopled with shadowy forms, while the throb-
bing activities of the second half are still present, as our
hands reach forth in guidance of the hesitating steps now
crossing the threshold of new endeavor.

> "The more we live, more brief appear
> Our life's succeeding stages;
> A day to childhood seems a year,
> And years like passing ages."

To the youth *looking forward,* in the rosy glow of the
morning and from the vantage-ground possessed by my
interesting audience, the busy world holds much that
attracts, while its difficulties are masked under a misty
film that half conceals, half reveals, but which the earnest
vitality of the novice attacks with confidence to brush
aside and press on to great achievement.

With adequate equipment, difficulties are overcome, but

in the preparation for the encounter many essentials may be overlooked, or their value miscalculated, and the struggling combatant finds, too late, his competitors, better prepared, meeting conditions and answering problems in a way that chagrins and disappoints. "And are there still new worlds to conquer?" asks our young Alexander.

In the field of *discovery*, what of the frozen North, the pathways blazed by Melville, Greely, Peary, Nansen, and the Yukon's icy steeps of golden promise? And of *invention*. Have the ends of the earth been united in vain over land and beneath seas by Morse, Edison, Tesla? And in *mechanics*. Is the list complete with Ericsson, Westinghouse, and Maxim; in ship-building and locomotives with Cramps and Baldwins? And will *statesmanship* halt and hesitate after Seward and Blaine and Reed? Is *literature* a lost art, embalmed in Hawthorne, Whittier, Longfellow, and Lowell? Hear Longfellow's voice:

> " Where are the stately argosies of song?
> Perhaps there lives some dreamy boy, untaught
> In schools, some graduate of the field or street
> Who shall become a master of the art,
> An admiral sailing the high seas of thought,
> Fearless and first and steering with his fleet
> For lands not yet laid down in any chart."

In the wise bounty of Stephen Girard, none of the great essentials for life work have been omitted, and the generations of lads who have enjoyed the fostering care of his College, so nobly founded, have received their training and tuition from a corps of instructors whose conscientious efforts not only instilled those "pure principles of morality and justice" that he esteemed so highly, but whose example of right living taught those broader views of upright manhood that were to give the after blessing.

> " Large was his bounty, and his soul sincere,
> Heaven did a recompense as largely send ;
> He gave to misery (all he had) a **tear** ;
> He gained **from Heaven** ('twas all he wish'd) a friend.''

To the care-worn business man, under the merciless rays of the mid-day sun, or in the quiet light of the evening hour, a *look backward* brings to mind much that yields a glint of pleasure and some results gained under pressure of duty alone, whose recompense ennobles; but the average success attained by the right use of the training so liberally bestowed carries its own reward in that " contentment which is great gain."

Shall the crowding competitions of life hold no cheer for those who " cross the great divide and face the setting sun"? Surely the great names of laurel-crowned memory lacked not length of days or strength of years by reason of duty well done or lasting achievement! And yon monument of chiselled stone, with its threescore names of lusty youth, who answered the bugle call to duty, records a noble sacrifice laid upon our country's altar; while its civic pride has not failed in lists of loyal manhood.

Can those who *look forward* from the protecting and sheltering walls of this Institution afford to forget the benefaction, the precepts and examples of the benefactor? And can we, who are passing the meridian, *look backward* without a kindling of the eye and quicker beating of heart-throbs in grateful recognition of his all-pervading and satisfying wisdom?

> " Let us, then, be up and doing,
> With a heart for any fate ;
> Still achieving, still pursuing,
> Learn to labor and to **wait**.''

EXERCISES—8 P.M.

GIRARD COLLEGE. CHAPEL AND BUILDING NO. 10.

PRAYER

BY BENJAMIN B. COMEGYS, ESQ.,

Of the Board of Directors of City Trusts.

(Selected from the Manual of the Chapel of Girard College.)

———————

Our Father, who art in heaven, Hallowed be thy name. Thy kingdom come. Thy will be done on earth, as it is in heaven. Give us this day our daily bread. And forgive us our trespasses, as we forgive those who trespass against us. And lead us not into temptation; but deliver us from evil: For thine is the kingdom, and the power, and the glory, for ever. Amen.

O Lord our God, we thank Thee for our lives, and all the gifts of grace and nature; for instruction in divine truth; for the voice of Thy calling, repeated so often; for Thy patience, Thy long-suffering towards us, who have so often and so grievously sinned against Thee; for all the benefits we have received; for any good we may have done; for the enjoyment of present good; for Thy promise and our hope of good to come; for wise teachers; for benefactors never to be forgotten; for brethren of one mind with us; for kind friends; for all who, by their writings or examples, have helped us on our way. For all these mercies, and for all others known or unknown, remembered or forgotten, we would bless and praise Thee now and forever.

Most merciful Father, we render thanks to Thee for

59

providing the means for our maintenance and instruction. We thank Thee that Thou didst move the Founder of this Institution to bequeath his wealth for its endowment. May we cherish the memory of his beneficence, and the gratitude we owe to him, who was an instrument in Thy hands for our good. On this anniversary of the opening of his College may we form new and stronger resolutions, to live in a manner worthy of our privileges; to improve our time and opportunities, and be prepared for useful and happy lives.

May we imitate the example of our benefactor in his industry, his honesty, his temperance, his public spirit, and in all parts of his conduct and character which were in accordance with Thy holy will.

O God, who seest that we have no power of ourselves, that we are not wise enough for our own direction, nor strong enough for our own defence, help us to acknowledge Thee in all our ways, so that we may not lean on our own understanding. Let Thy light guide us, Thy providence protect us, Thy grace help us faithfully to discharge all our duties; that, being armed with Thy defence, we may be preserved from all dangers.

Blessed Lord, who hast given us a new commandment that we should love one another, and hast taught us that where envy and strife are there is confusion, and every evil work; give us grace, that we may be kindly affectioned one to another. Help us to put away all bitterness, and wrath, and anger, and evil speaking, with all malice; and grant that, in honor preferring one another, we may walk in love, even as Thou, Lord, didst love us.

O Lord God, the Life of mortals, the Light of the faithful, the Strength of those who labor, and the Repose of

the blessed dead, grant us a peaceful night, free from all
disturbance, that after an interval of quiet sleep we may by
Thy bounty, at the retùrn of light, be endued with activity,
and enabled in security to render thanks to Thee; through
Jesus Christ our Lord.

Almighty God, who hast given us grace at this time
with one accord to make our common supplications unto
Thee; and dost promise that when two or three are
gathered together in Thy name Thou wilt grant their re-
quests; fulfil now, O Lord, the desires and petitions of
Thy servants, as may be most expedient for us; grant-
ing us in this world knowledge of Thy truth, and in the
world to come life everlasting.   Amen.

INTRODUCTORY REMARKS

BY GENERAL LOUIS WAGNER,

President of the Board of Directors of City **Trusts.**

·

LADIES AND GENTLEMEN:—The records show that on January 1, 1848 (fifty years ago to a day on Saturday last), there were assembled in the room in the southwest corner of the Main Building, then the chapel of Girard College, but now containing Mr. Girard's personal effects, and known as the Memorial Room, "the Councils of the City, and other City, County and State officers, and numerous citizens," "and the College was opened with a few simple exercises, suited to the character of the Institution."

Mr. Joseph R. Chandler, one of the leading citizens of Philadelphia in his day and generation, as President of the Board of Directors, addressed those assembled in words well fitting the time and place. He congratulated them upon the final accomplishment of "the object for which the community had so long waited and for which some present had so constantly labored," explained the details adopted for putting into practical operation the long-delayed plans of the testator, and expressed the hope that the results of the institution would justify their expectations.

Concluding his address, he introduced the Hon. Joel Jones, the President of the College, who, in well-chosen

words, emphasized the suggestions of Mr. Chandler and briefly outlined the general scope of the College. In the course of his remarks he said,—

" Fellow-citizens, we are about to enter upon the execution of a scheme of education in some respects new and difficult, but in every respect important. The foundation of it is a charity,—munificent in its provisions, comprehensive and noble in its objects, and far-reaching in its results. Should it merely fail, we suffer the loss of a great good; should it ever be perverted, we may incur great evils. But should it be made to accomplish the benevolent designs of the Founder of the College, we shall secure to many orphans a better inheritance than riches."

And, finally, he said,—

" And now the question comes, Shall this noble design, for which the late Mr. Girard has made so large provision, be realized? Shall these beautiful and enduring walls become the mausoleum of his hopes, or the emblem of a yet more enduring and more beautiful moral and intellectual structure?"

And now, half a century after, you, as the Councils and other officers of City and State, and you, as the representative citizens of Philadelphia and vicinity, and we, as the successors of the then Board of Directors of the College, assemble in this larger hall to inquire of the past and to plan for the future.

Has Mr. Girard's noble design been realized, or has it failed of its purposes? Have "these beautiful and enduring walls become the mausoleum of his hopes, or the emblem of a yet more enduring and more beautiful moral and intellectual structure"?

As Chairman of this meeting, it is clearly not in my

province, nor would it be in good taste, for me to trespass upon the time of the regular speakers of the evening to attempt a reply to these questions; but an active connection with the affairs of Girard College since the first Monday of January, 1867, thirty-one years ago to-day, when I was appointed a member of the Committee of City Councils having charge of the affairs of the Girard Estate, both tempts me and enables me to say that the results of the past fifty years show ability in instruction, intelligence in management, integrity in administration, and always fidelity to Mr. Girard's plans as laid down in his will.

From 100 pupils in 1848 we have increased to over 1500,—five times as many as named by Mr. Girard as the number for which the College was originally planned. Nearly 6000 have been admitted into the College; 4500 have become part of the busy outside world, making their impress upon City, Commonwealth and Nation.

The endowment fund has increased from an estimated value of $5,000,000 to an estimated value of $26,000,000, and $15,000,000 have been expended in the maintenance and enlargement of the College.

Surely these figures show that, numerically and financially, Mr. Girard's plans have not failed, and the thousands of young men, graduates of his College, who rise up and call him blessed, evidence by ability and character that they have secured "a better inheritance than riches."

With such a retrospect, what a glorious prospect!

With a trust magnificently endowed, with a charity the grandest in the world, with the record of fifty years unparalleled by any public trust anywhere, let us all—you, as citizens and officers of State and Nation, and we, as the immediate administrators of Mr. Girard's will, but, above all, you, as the present and former recipients of his bounty —see to it that that which has come down to us in such grand proportions shall suffer no harm in our day, so that its blessings may continue to increase and to multiply to the end of time.

HISTORICAL ADDRESS

BY ADAM H. FETTEROLF, PH.D., LL.D.,

President of Girard College.

In the short time that I shall occupy your attention this evening, I shall not attempt to give anything like a connected history of Girard College. The story of fifty years cannot be told in a brief address. I shall endeavor to notice only a few of the most important features and events; for particulars and statistics I must refer you to the printed page.

When, on the day following Christmas in 1831, Philadelphia's most distinguished man and citizen, Stephen Girard, passed away, there arose in the minds of the community two questions: first, what is his estate? and, second, what disposition has he made of it? His great wealth had brought him great fame. Being the first millionaire that America had produced, he was naturally an object of great interest and curiosity. Presidents and ex-Presidents of the United States were more familiar figures in public than were millionaires in Mr. Girard's day. The great banker had not only a vast fortune of his own, but he had also a mind of his own. In nothing was this more manifest than in his last will and testament. The same keen foresight and singleness of purpose which he displayed in the accumulation of his wealth are shown in the disposition of it. He saw where it would do the most

66

GIRARD COLLEGE.   BUILDING NO. 8.

good, and there he placed it. It was the thought and purpose of his later years to assist those beginning life with
the tide of fortune at the ebb, that they might have a
better home and a better training than they would receive
from the application of the public funds. It was the same
spirit which showed itself brave and humane in time of
plague, public-spirited and patriotic in time of financial
distress. The famous will was written by William J.
Duane, of the Philadelphia Bar. When the document
was finally executed, the lawyer said to the testator, "It
will not stand." "Yes, it will," replied the testator, and
time has proved which was right.

The work of erecting the first five buildings was begun
in 1833, the corner-stone being laid with appropriate ceremonies on July 4 of that year. A most impressive address
was delivered on the occasion by Mr. Nicholas Biddle,
a distinguished member of a distinguished family. The
original establishment, consisting of the Main Building
and the two buildings on either side, was completed and
formally presented to the Directors in November, 1847,
and the College opened on January 1 of the ensuing year.

It may not be generally known that an effort was made
to organize for the purpose of instruction in 1838, ten
years before the College was actually opened.

In 1836, the Trustees, with the authority of the City
Councils, appointed a president of the College in the person of Alexander Dallas Bache, Professor of Natural
Philosophy in the University of Pennsylvania, who immediately sailed for Europe to examine similar institutions abroad, and to purchase books and apparatus. On
the return of Professor Bache, two years later, the Trustees
were suddenly and unexpectedly informed by the Com-

missioners of the Girard Estate that their counsel, John
Sergeant, had decided that the duties of the College could
not begin until the whole was completed. This was a
great surprise and no little embarrassment to the Trustees,
and a sad disappointment to the people of the city. The
President-elect, after publishing a voluminous report of
his visit to Europe, returned to his professorship in the
University, and in 1843 became Superintendent of the
Coast Survey.

A word of praise is due the architect of the first College
buildings, Mr. Thomas U. Walter. His task was not an
easy one. He had in this country no precedent. He built
the first Grecian temple in the United States, and the finest
specimen in existence at the present day. He was obliged
to serve a building committee the membership of which
was constantly changing under the system of making appointments then in vogue. And yet we find in every annual report of the committee none but words of praise for
the architect. They uniformly commend the skill, good
taste and faithfulness with which he managed this colossal
work. He had the community to please also. People
were impatient to see the great College completed, and
during the progress of the work there were many and constant complaints and expressions of impatience. Even
Charles Dickens, in his " American Notes," takes occasion
to criticise the American people for not hurrying to completion the gigantic structure. He says, " Near the city
is a most splendid unfinished marble structure for the
Girard College, founded by a deceased gentleman of that
name, and of enormous wealth, which, if completed according to the original design, will be perhaps the richest
edifice of modern times. But the bequest is involved in

legal disputes, and pending them the work has stopped; so that, like many other great undertakings in America, even this is rather going to be done one of these days, than doing now."

One of the chief causes of delay was the scarcity of skilled workmen. At one time the building committee advertised for stone-cutters in Boston, New York and Baltimore, and the result was the accession of only three men.

But notwithstanding the many and unavoidable delays and interruptions in the work, probably never before was there a building of such size and finish constructed as rapidly as our Main Building. The Church of the Madeleine, in Paris, of similar architecture, and perhaps equal to it in magnitude, was twenty-seven years in building, not including the time when, on account of national troubles, all such operations were suspended in the French capital.

It is a matter of some interest that, while Mr. Girard was most explicit in the details of the several structures, he does not mention the portico of the Main Building. As this addition involved an outlay of several hundred thousand dollars, there was much criticism, and the building committee were charged with extravagance. The committee in their final report say, "There is nothing that could have been omitted, except the surrounding portico; and that is fully justified, if not required, by the injunction of Mr. Girard, that 'utility and good taste should be left to determine in the particulars not specified in the will.' This portico was adopted by Councils after great deliberation, and with singular unanimity; and it only remains for those who object, to look at the building and say whether

5

it would have been a tasteful object had the proportions given by Mr. Girard been adhered to, and the surrounding portico omitted."

The order of architecture has often been commented upon and criticised on the ground that expense might have been avoided if an order less ornate had been chosen. Both the architect and building committee declare that the Corinthian style was chosen for the sake of economy alone. The plan and general style having once been decided upon, it was necessary to choose one of the three Grecian orders,—the Doric, Ionic or Corinthian. Of these, the last named was the least expensive. A Doric column capable of reaching so high would have required a thickness of nine and a half feet, which would have made it cost twice as much as one of the Corinthian columns. The Ionic order, in like manner, would have demanded a thicker shaft, and capitals carved from a single block of marble.

The most important event between the time of laying the corner-stone and the opening of the College was the famous Girard Will Contest. The heirs-at-law instituted a suit in 1836. The case did not come up for hearing until six years later, when it was decided in favor of the will. It was argued in the Supreme Court in 1843; a rehearing ordered, and again argued the following year, Daniel Webster having in the mean time been retained by the heirs. Mr. Webster realized that he had a weak case in point of law, but he readily detected a method by which he could go boldly outside the law, and substitute for argument "an impassioned appeal to emotion and prejudice."

Webster's plea was for the Christian Religion, and so powerful was the speech in its eulogy and defence, that the people of Washington, irrespective of denomination, held a meeting, and appointed a committee to wait on Mr. Webster and ask permission to have his address printed. He gave his assent, and it was afterwards published and widely disseminated.

The plea was eloquent, sentimental and even pathetic. But eloquence, sentiment and pathos are not argument. Webster failed to prove that Girard College must of necessity be an anti-Christian institution, and the Supreme Court decided unanimously in favor of the will and the College. Chief Justice Story ruled that an institution may be Christian without being sectarian, and that there could be religious instruction even though the minister, missionary and ecclesiastic be excluded.

The lawyers for the will were John Sergeant and Horace Binney, of the Philadelphia Bar, and with such signal ability and learning did they conduct their case, that President Tyler was moved to confer a seat on the Supreme Bench first to Mr. Sergeant and then to Mr. Binney, an honor which they both declined.

As early as 1833, the idea suggested itself to the minds of prominent citizens of Philadelphia that Girard's remains should repose in Girard's college. In the same year the building committee were authorized by Councils to construct a vault in the Main Building, in the most suitable and durable manner, and were further directed to transfer the remains thither as soon as might be. It was not, however, until 1851, eighteen years later, that the body of the Founder was brought to the Institution. The occasion was a great civic pageant, and was conducted entirely by the Masonic Order. The procession was one of the largest of its kind ever seen in the city, the number of

Masons in line being over fifteen hundred. The remains were deposited in the south vestibule of the Main Building, in the marble sarcophagus where they still repose.

On January 1, 1848, there assembled in the old chapel, which is now the Memorial Room, the directors, teachers, officers and pupils of the Girard College. There were sixteen directors, seventeen officers and teachers, and one hundred pupils. These constituted the College at its first opening. Of the sixteen directors, only one survives,—Mr. Frederick Fraley. Of the teachers, Miss Mary Lynch, who died June 22, 1897, was the last to pass away. All the other officers—president, matron, steward and teachers —have gone to their reward.

As no boy could be admitted over ten years of age, the College was at first a school for children,—an elementary school. There was no need of a college department, since there were no boys ready for college instruction. As the boys grew in years, the demand for higher instruction grew, and the upper forms became a necessity. The first complete curriculum was adopted in 1853, and the first class was graduated in 1854.

The number of boys has grown from one hundred in January, 1848, to fifteen hundred and thirty-six in January, 1898. The buildings have increased from five to fourteen, and the staff of teachers and officers from seventeen to one hundred and fifteen.

The number of teachers and officers connected with the College since its opening is 349; pupils, 5,899.

There have been but four Presidents of the College. At the opening in 1848, the Hon. Joel Jones, formerly a judge of the Court of Common Pleas in Philadelphia, was elected to the position, but remained in charge less than

GIRARD COLLEGE.   DINING ROOM, BUILDING NO. 8.

two years. He was succeeded in 1850 by Dr. William H. Allen, then a professor in Dickinson College. With the exception of an interval of four years,—from 1863 to 1867, when Major Richard Somers Smith, a graduate of West Point, was the executive,—he remained in the presidency until his death in 1882. No one could have been better fitted for this office by natural temperament and training than Dr. Allen. With fine presence, superior talents, genial disposition, and rare executive ability, he was peculiarly adapted for the labors and responsibilities of a position the duties of which are so many and so varied. The chancel window of this chapel bears testimony to the regard and esteem in which he was held by the Alumni of the College.

There have been also four Vice-Presidents of the College since the position was first created in 1877. Henry W. Arey, A.M., Adam H. Fetterolf, LL.D., Henry D. Gregory, LL.D., and Winthrop D. Sheldon, A.M., the present incumbent.

In fulfilling the plans of its Founder, the College has three purposes in view. First, to provide for the orphan wards of the city of Philadelphia a comfortable and happy home, in which their health and physical welfare shall be duly cared for, so that they may grow up to a sound and vigorous manhood; second, to furnish such education of head and hand as shall prepare them for intelligent and industrious citizenship; and third, to give them such training in all the essentials of character as shall fit them to be upright, law-abiding and useful members of the community in which they may hereafter dwell. To accomplish these objects, the College was organized and is carried on.

In directing what branches should be taught, the

Founder designates but does not restrict. The will on this point is liberal and comprehensive, and, like the Constitution of the United States, has its elastic clause, namely, " I would have them taught facts and things rather than words and signs." Under this provision, the course of study has been often extended and revised to meet the demands of experience, and to keep abreast with the times and current progress in education. The last fifty years cover a period of great educational awakening. There have been so many changes, that we have come to speak of the education of the present day as the new education. Yet these changes have not, in every instance, meant improvements. Many experiments have proved failures. In speaking of this subject, our learned Commissioner of Education, Dr. William T. Harris, says, " Experiments are so costly that one must be cautious in undertaking them. Ninety-nine fail and one succeeds." Our policy has been to keep well abreast of the times, and to take up with a new idea, not because it is new, but because it is good; and to give up old methods and old systems, not because they are old, but because they are no longer the best.

The boys of the Girard College need a practical training. They need, in addition to knowledge and intelligence, skill and efficiency. They must have that which will enable them to earn their livelihood as soon as they leave school. For this reason, we have always endeavored to teach all our pupils to do everything with thoroughness and accuracy. In all grades, special emphasis is placed upon those studies which will directly prepare the pupil for efficient service in that class of pursuits into which he will enter. At the same time, it is steadily kept in view

that education is not merely a preparation for bread-win-
ning, but is far more than this,—a preparation for broad,
generous, useful life,—for living itself.

The corner-stone was laid on July 4, 1833, precisely at
the hour of noon. It was a happy thought that such an
event should be celebrated on Independence Day. It
suggested patriotism as one of the cardinal virtues to be
kept before the minds of the youth who come here to be
educated; the same thought that the Founder had in mind
when in his will he directs that "by every proper means a
pure attachment to our republican institutions should be
formed and fostered in the minds of the scholars." And
every one familiar with the College will bear testimony
that a more patriotic company of boys than those who are
gathered from time to time within the College enclosure
cannot be found anywhere. Love for the flag, respect and
veneration for our patriotic soldiers and statesmen, and
loyalty to the government that protects them, are always
before their minds. This, with the efficient military training which they are constantly receiving, makes them citizens upon whom the government can depend to do honest
and intelligent voting in time of peace, and brave fighting
in time of war. The Soldiers' Monument, standing within
the grounds, unveiled in 1869, bears testimony to the fact
that Girard College patriotism is not sentiment only. At
the breaking out of the war, about three hundred boys had
left the College. How many of these enlisted we do not
exactly know, but the monument bears record that at least
twenty-five gave their lives for their country.

Under the will of the Founder, the boys on leaving the
College are to be "bound out" "to suitable occupations,
as those of agriculture, navigation and mechanical trades,

arts and manufactures." While the old apprentice system which obtained in Mr. Girard's time was a help and a convenience in the early history of the College, it gradually became a serious hinderance. Employers refused to enter into the obligation of master, and the average boy disliked the idea of being an indentured apprentice bound to an employer for a definite number of years; so that binding out grew more and more into disfavor, until it finally became a question of whether we should give up the apprenticing, or close to our boys many avenues of business offering the best opportunities for bright and energetic lads. The Board of Directors wisely chose the former alternative. Under our present system, when a boy has found suitable employment, or has reached the age when the authorities think he should no longer remain in the Institution, his college indenture is cancelled, and he is returned to his mother or next friend. While we consider ourselves thus legally relieved from all responsibility, we still keep an oversight over the boy until he becomes twenty-one years of age. Our Superintendent of Admission and Indentures visits, as far as he is able, all boys under twenty-one years of age at least once a year.

The gentlemen who, from time to time, have had the responsibility of directing the affairs of the College and of the Girard Estate have ever been the best of the city,—men distinguished for their intelligence, integrity and good business judgment. For the first twenty-two years, the Trust was administered by a board of sixteen directors chosen by the City Councils,—four being appointed each year. A serious objection to this system of appointment was the short and uncertain tenure of office, and a lack of permanency and stability in a body having to make many and important business contracts. During the twenty-two years that this system obtained, there were on the board of management ninety-five different directors,— each having served an average of four years.

An act creating the present Board of Directors of City Trusts was approved by the Governor on the thirtieth day of June, 1869, and the first board was appointed two months later. The City Councils refused to acknowledge the right of the new board, and an appeal was made to the courts to test the validity of the act of the Legislature creating it. Justice Sherwood delivered the unanimous opinion of the court affirming the validity of the law. The city then withdrew its opposition, and the new board took charge February 25, 1870. Under the existing system there have been in twenty-eight years twenty-seven members, and the average term of service twelve years.

Under their management, the Residuary Fund has increased one hundred per cent., and the net income two hundred per cent. There has been a general improved condition of the grounds and buildings, steam heating and electric lighting throughout, and a filtering plant by which our entire water supply is purified. In the educational work, the improvements of recent years include our manual training school, thoroughly equipped in all its departments, and ranking among the earliest and best in the country; the department of natural history, with its well selected museum; the addition of a laboratory to the course of chemistry and physics; our school of typewriting and shorthand, and the increase of our library, recently catalogued. We have also introduced, most successfully, systematic voice culture, with instruction in sight reading and part singing, calisthenics, military science and tactics, and thrift teaching, by which the boys are encouraged to put in a saving-fund the little sums of money given them from time to time. In this way we hope to foster the habit of saving, so important in the man and the citizen, in a country where waste and extravagance are so general.

What becomes of our boys? This is of all questions the most important. What is the College, with its munificent endowments, its stately buildings, and its grand equipment, doing for the lads entrusted to its care and training? We must estimate it, as we do a family, a community or a State, by the citizens it produces.

Count Bismarck says, " One-third of the students of the German universities destroy themselves by dissipation; one-third wear themselves out by overwork, and the rest govern Europe." President David Starr Jordan, of the Leland Stanford, Jr., University, in alluding to this statement of the distinguished German statesman, observes that while the numerical quality of these three classes cannot be insisted upon, we still recognize that something of this sort is true of the college students of America, adding that, " One part ' go to the dogs,' one part go to the grave, and the rest are the strength of the Republic." This is a rather startling statement, and if true, a sad one,—that only one-third of the young men who attend the universities and colleges are saved to live a life of usefulness.

The Girard boy is neither born great, nor does he have greatness thrust upon him. His greatness is his own achievement. When he leaves his Alma Mater, he must at once earn his own living. This may be a hardship, but not a misfortune.

During the last two months we have been trying, with the assistance of a Committee of the Alumni, to collect in-

formation as to how many of the graduates are living and
how they have prospered. While the statistics are still far
from being complete, they are very valuable in enabling
us to see the results of the training boys have received
while in the College.

The occupations they have taken up are about as varied
as would be those of the same number of boys going out
from the public schools. About thirty per cent. are engaged
in mechanical or kindred pursuits. Some have entered
the professions. Some have become successful journalists,
while others have held high official positions in the city,
the State and the nation. Fully ninety per cent. are doing,
and have done, credit to themselves and their early home.
After an experience of seventeen years with the boys of
Girard College, I have been convinced that no lads go out
into life with better ideals. They have no other thought
than that of winning their own way, to do and be that
which makes sterling manhood and good citizenship. It
is the boast of the famous Winchester School that it makes
good Englishmen. Girard College claims that it makes
good Americans.

For over a dozen years, our Superintendent of Admission and Indentures has been visiting, mingling and consulting with the boys and young men who have gone out
of the College to take their places in the world as workers,
voters and thinkers. His reports are uniformly of an en-
couraging character. He speaks of the Girard boy as
ambitious, honest and diligent. Ambitious to succeed in
their vocation; honest in their dealings and intercourse
with their fellows, and diligent in the discharge of duty.
He reports them as kind and affectionate in the family,

faithful and devoted in their religious work, and ever loyal in their attachment to our republican institutions.

Of the older Alumni who have reached the years of manhood, we may be justly proud. They are Girard's greatest, because his living, monument. They are to be met with in all the walks of life, and invariably among our best citizens.

In conclusion, it is not to be forgotten that Stephen Girard did more than establish Girard College,—he established a precedent. As the first of our large givers, he taught men that wealth, like life itself, is opportunity. His example has had many distinguished followers, who have learned from him the noble lesson that the greatest privilege of living is that of doing good to our fellow-men.

Girard College as compared with the famous schools of the old world is yet in its infancy. What its work and influence in the future may be can only be imagined. During the centuries and ages to follow, boys will continue to come to these halls to be trained for duty and for living, —to be men and to be citizens. Those who are now directing and teaching will gradually drop out and others will step in and take their places.

May each half-century be a half-century of progress, each accomplish better and nobler things than that which has gone before. And may others

> " Finish what we begin
> And all that we fail of, win."

GIRARD COLLEGE.   BUILDING NO. 9.

ADDRESS

BY HON. THOMAS B. REED,

Speaker of the House of Representatives.

Six hundred and fifty or seventy years ago, England, which, during the following period of nearly seven centuries, has been the richest nation on the face of the globe, began to establish the two great universities which, from the banks of the Cam and the Isis, have sent forth great scholars and priests and statesmen whose fame is the history of their own country, and whose deeds have been part of the history of every land and sea. During all that long period, reaching back two hundred and fifty years before it was even dreamed that this great hemisphere existed, before the world knew that it was swinging in the air and rolling about the sun, kings and cardinals, nobles and great churchmen, the learned and the pious, began bestowing upon those abodes of scholars their gifts of land and money, and they have continued their benefactions down to our time. What those universities, with all their colleges and halls teeming with scholars for six hundred years, have done for the progress of civilization and the good of man this whole evening could not begin to tell. Even your imaginations cannot, at this moment, create the surprising picture. Nevertheless, the Institution at which most of you are, or have been, pupils is at the beginning of a career with which those great uni-

versities and their great history may struggle in vain for
the palm of the greatest usefulness to the race of man.
One single fact will make it evident that this possibility
is not the creation of imagination or the product of that
boastfulness which America will some day feel herself too
great to cherish, but a simple and plain possibility which
has the sanction of mathematics as well as hope.

Although more than six centuries of regal, princely, and
pious donations have been poured into the purses of these
venerable aids to learning, the munificence of one American citizen to-day affords an endowment income equal to
that of each university, and when the full century has completed his work will afford an income superior to the
income of both. When Time has done his perfect work,
Stephen Girard, mariner and merchant, may be found to
have come nearer immortality than the long procession
of kings and cardinals, nobles and statesmen, whose power
was mighty in their own days, but who are only on their
way to oblivion. I am well aware that this College of
Orphans, wherein the wisdom of the Founder requires
facts and things to be taught rather than words and signs,
can as yet make no claim to that higher learning so essential to the ultimate progress of the world; but it has its
own mission as great and as high, and one which connects
itself more nearly with the practical elevation of mankind.

Whether the overruling Providence, of which we talk
so much and know so little, has each of us in His kindly
care and keeping, we shall better know when our minds
have the broader scope which immortality will make possible. But, however men may dispute over individual
care, His care over the race as a whole fills all the pages
of human history. Unity and progress are the watch-

words of the Divine guidance, and no matter how harsh
has been the treatment by one man of thousands of men,
every great event, or series of events, has been for the
good of the race. Were this the proper time, I could show
that wars—and wars ought to be banished forever from
the face of the earth; that pestilences—and the time is
coming when they will be no more; that persecutions and
inquisitions—and liberty of thought is the richest pearl of
life,—that all these things—wars, pestilences and persecutions—were but helps to the unity of mankind. All things,
including our own natures, bind us together for deep and
unrelenting purpose.

Think what we should be, who are unlearned and
brutish, if the wise, the learned, and the good could separate themselves from us; were free from our superstitions
and vague and foolish fears, and stood loftily by themselves, wrapped in their own superior wisdom. Therefore
hath it been wisely ordained that no set of creatures of our
race shall be beyond the reach of their helping hand; so
lofty that they will not fear our reproaches, or so mighty as
to be beyond our reach. If the lofty and the learned do not
lift us up, we drag them down. But unity is not the only
watchword; there must be progress also. Since, by a law
we cannot evade, we are to keep together, and since we
are to progress, we must do it together, and nobody must
be left behind. This is not a matter of philosophy; it is
a matter of fact. No progress which did not lift all, ever
lifted any. If we let the poison of filth diseases percolate
through the hovels of the poor, death knocks at the palace
gates. If we leave to the greater horror of ignorance any
portion of our race, the consequences of ignorance strike
us all, and there is no escape. We must all move, but we

must all keep together. It is only when the rear-guard comes up that the vanguard can go on.

Stephen Girard must have understood this. He took under his charge the progress of those who needed his aid, knowing that if they were added to the list of good citizens, to the catalogue of moral, enterprising, and useful men, there was so much added, not to their happiness only, but to the welfare of the race to which he belonged. For his orphans the vanguard need not wait. Your Founder also understood what education was. Most men brought up as he was on shipboard and on shore, with few books and fewer studies, if they cared for learning at all, would have had for learning an uncouth reverence, such as the savage has for his idol, a reverence for the fancied magnificence of the unknown. This would have led him to establish a university devoted to out-of-the-way learning beyond his ken, or to link his name to glories to which he could not aspire. But the man who named his vessels after the great French authors of his age, and who read their works himself, knew from them, and from his own laborious and successful life, that learning was not all of education, and so gave his orphans an entrance into a practical world with such learning as left the whole field of learning before them, if they wanted it, with power to make fortunes besides.

It is strange to watch the growth into fame and respect and reverence of Stephen Girard as his plan of conferring a benefaction upon the city and the people whom he has loved has slowly unfolded itself before their gaze. The generation in which he lives can seldom understand the really great man. We live for to-day, and he lives for a day after to-day. He takes on the century in which he lives and a hundred years after he has passed away. The man of mediocrity must make his hay under the shine of the present sun, and so must clasp every hand he can touch and make us think he loves us all. But the greatest merchant of his time, with the noblest ambition of them all, was so resolute in his pursuit of wealth, and so coldly determined in all his endeavors, that he seems to have uncovered to few or to none the generous purpose of his heart. What he said to the man who was so unworthy to write his first biography, but who was forced to bless when he had gone forth to curse, is the secret of his career. " My actions must make my life," he said, and of his life not one moment was wasted. "Facts and things rather than words and signs" were the warp and woof of his existence. No wonder he left the injunction that this should be the teaching of those objects of his bounty into whose faces he was never to look.

The vast wealth which Mr. Girard had was of itself alone evidence of greatness.

I have not forgotten the epitaph on Colonel Charters, who died rich and infamous, that you could see what God thought of riches by the people He gave them to. Fortunes may be made and lost. Fortunes may be inherited. These things mean nothing. But the fortune which has given us all our surroundings to-night was made and firmly held in a hand of eighty years. That meant greatness. But when the dead hand opens and pours the rich bloom of a preparation for life over six thousand boys in the half-century which has gone and thousands in the centuries to come, that means more than greatness. Mr. Girard gave more than his money. He put into his enter-

6

prise his own powerful brain, and, like the ships he sent to sea, long after his death the adventure came home laden, not with the results of his capital alone, but of his forethought and his genius. He builded for so many years that the stars will be cold before his work is finished. We envious people, who cannot be wealthy any more than we can add a cubit to our stature, avenge ourselves by thinking and proclaiming that pursuit of wealth is sordid and stifles the nobler sentiments of the soul. Whether this be so or not, if whoever makes to grow two blades of grass where but one grew before is a benefactor of his race, he also is a benefactor who makes two ships sail the sea where but one encountered its storms before. However sordid the owner may be, this is a benefit of which he cannot deprive the world.

That men who have achieved great riches are not always shut out by their riches from the nobler emotions, Stephen Girard was himself a most illustrious example. A hundred years ago this city was under the black horror of a plague. So terrible was the fear that fell upon the city, that the tenderest of domestic ties—the love of husband and wife and of parents for children—seemed obliterated. Even gold lost its power in the multitudinous presence of impending death. There was no refuge even in the hospital, which, reeking with disease, was a hell out of which there was no redemption. Neither money nor affection could buy service. "Fear was on every soul."

Mr. Girard was then in the prime of life, forty-two years old, in health and strength, already rich, and with a future as secure as ever falls to human lot. Of his own accord, as a volunteer, he took charge of the interior of the deadly hospital, and for two long and weary months stood face to face with death.

A poet himself has sung in vain of what makes the little songs linger in our hearts for ages, while epics perish and tragedies pass out of sight. Why this is so we shall never know by reason alone. Way down in the human heart there is a tenderness for self-sacrifice which makes it seem loftier than the love of glory, and reveals the possibility of the eternal soul.

Wars and sieges pass away and great intellectual efforts cease to stir our hearts, but the man who sacrifices himself for his fellow lives forever.

We forget the war in which was the siege of Zutphen, and almost the city itself, but we shall never forget the death of Sir Philip Sidney. Scholars alone read the work of his life, but all mankind honors him in the story of his death. The great war of the Crimea, in our own day, with its generals and marshals, and its bands of storming soldiery, has almost passed from our memories, but the time will never come when the charge of Balaklava will cease to stir the heart or pass from story or from song. It happened to Stephen Girard, mariner and merchant, seeking wealth and finding it, whose ships covered every sea, whose intellect penetrated, as your treasurer's books will show, a hundred years into the future, to light up his life by a deed more noble than the dying courtesy of Sidney and braver than the charge of the six hundred, for he walked under his own orders day by day and week by week, shoulder to shoulder with death, and was not afraid. How fit, indeed, it is that amidst these temples which are the tribute to his intellect should stand the tablet which is the tribute to his heart!

Surely, if the immortal dead, serene with the wisdom of eternity, are not above all joy and pride, he must feel a thrill to know that no mariner or merchant ever sent forth a venture upon unknown seas which came back with richer cargoes or in statelier ships.

REMARKS BY THE CHAIRMAN

General Wagner prefaced his remarks with the following:

I will read at this time a telegram from Governor Hastings:

"I deeply regret that annual meetings of banking and other interests, postponed from Saturday, make it impossible for me to leave here to-day. I hope you will appreciate my disappointment at not being able to be present at the Stephen Girard semi-centennial, and to greet the alumni and management of the noblest benefaction in this country."

We anticipated great pleasure in having the Governor of the Commonwealth with us, more particularly as the first graduate of the Institution, Mr. George W. Jackson, was a partner of his in business at Bellefonte; and we had expected to hear from the Governor of his personal knowledge of the results of the education and training at Girard College.

Governor Hastings is not here, but in his place we have captured a speaker who will, I am certain, when the proper point in the programme is reached, interest and instruct us. Who he is I will tell you after a while.

President Fetterolf referred to the fact that Mr. Frederick Fraley, our oldest and most distinguished citizen of Philadelphia, one of the first Directors of the College, still lives. We invited him to be present with us, and he writes

89

that physical inability prevents, concluding his letter as follows:

"Among the most precious of my memories are the years of my official connection with the Girard College. And now, as the only survivor of the Board of Directors of 1847 and 1848, I am thankful that I have been permitted to live until its fiftieth anniversary.

"Faithfully yours,

"FREDERICK FRALEY."

General Wagner then introduced the next speaker in the following remarks:

Now, I want to tell you a very brief story. When the committee having charge of these exercises cast about for speakers, they said, "We want Reed." And we have him. They then looked for the proper man to make us the second address. We said we wanted a college president; and we wanted the president from the college at Easton. But somebody said, "He's a preacher, and he can't get in." That seemed to settle the case, of course; and we looked about, and finally concluded that the man in that capacity couldn't be had. We felt compelled to make other arrangements, and thought President Fetterolf had committed a frightful blunder when he sent a general invitation to the president of the college at Easton, who promptly accepted it.

Then we carefully examined the records, as we should have done at first, and found that the gentleman did not *preach* at all,—he *practised* (which is the more difficult); that his brother preached, but he did not; and of course we said to him, "We shall be glad to see you." And he is here. Then, when the telegram came that Governor Hastings could not be here, we laid violent hands upon this man who is not a preacher, and said, "Now, the speech that you would have had a month to prepare, we will give you, in addition to your dinner, fifteen minutes to get ready." Being a Presbyterian ruling elder, and not a preaching elder, he of course bowed to fate, took it for granted that it was foreordained, and said, " I submit."

More appropriate still. We are to-night celebrating the fiftieth anniversary of Girard College, an institution established by a native of France, but, as Speaker Reed has said, an American citizen from the crown of his head to the soles of his feet. And the gentleman who will now talk to us is the president of a college named after another native of France,—one who helped to establish the independence of the Colonies, and made possible these United States of America.

When I said that Governor Hastings would not be here, but that we had another speaker in reserve, somebody said, " Well, that's Brosius;" somebody else said, " That's MacVeagh;" others, " Loudon Snowden;" and I said quietly to myself, " You are all wrong; any one of these, or of a dozen others on the platform, could make a good speech at any time, yet none of these is the man we have captured."

I take great pleasure in presenting to you E. D. Warfield, LL.D., the President of Lafayette College.

ADDRESS

BY ETHELBERT D. WARFIELD, LL.D.,

President of Lafayette College.

MR. CHAIRMAN, LADIES AND GENTLEMEN:—It is very evident that we have another Presbyterian ruling elder here, and that he has been practising on this audience. I thought he would have a good deal of "nerve" who would dare to stand up before so large an assemblage of citizens of Pennsylvania and undertake to say which one of all that noble army of martyrs, too numerous to be named, who are reluctantly expecting to be called upon to take the place of Governor Hastings, is indeed the man.

I am only surprised that you have so readily acquiesced in his nomination. As a Presbyterian, I not only believe in foreordination, but also in "election." Hence I, too, must acquiesce in General Wagner's selection.

I can assure you, however, that I am not a preacher. I recall with approval the reply of an old darky down in Kentucky, who, when asked if he were not a preacher, replied, "Oh, no, young massa, I ain't no preacher; I is a 'zorter. You know a preacher is bound to stick to his text, but a 'zorter, he can branch." It is a very great privilege on such an occasion to be able to "branch," especially when you haven't a text. I looked on the programme, and I couldn't see what Governor Hastings, or I, or anybody else, was expected to talk about. So I

GIRARD COLLEGE. MANUAL TRAINING SCHOOL BUILDING.

thought that, in commemorating the great work of this College, its high moral attitude, or something of that sort, was surely in keeping with the occasion. Then I thought of the distinguished Frenchman who died a few days ago, and concerning whom we have been hearing so much in the newspapers,—Mr. Alphonse Daudet,—and I remembered a little incident connected with him when he came in contact with our American ideas of morality. You will recollect, perhaps, that when he was writing his novel, "Sapho," in which he undertook to teach his sons, and the French nation generally, sound morals, Messrs. Funk & Wagnalls, the eminent publishers of *The Voice* (a paper well known in connection with its interest in the morals of another college, which will not now be mentioned), heard that Mr. Daudet was about to publish a novel to teach morality, and contracted with him for the American rights of "Sapho." "Sapho" when finished was sent to them. Then Messrs. Funk & Wagnalls drank in draughts of morality, such as they are so constantly receiving from their special agents, and for once they must have reeled. We can scarcely suppose that they were intoxicated, but it was something a little stronger than they had been accustomed to imbibe as pure morality. So they cabled to Mr. Daudet, "'Sapho' will not do." Mr. Daudet was completely overcome at the idea that anything he wrote could be rejected. Therefore he hastened to an English friend, and asked him what on earth this meant. The friend looked at the cablegram, and said, "Why, it's perfectly plain. You French spell 'Sapho' with one 'p,' while the English spell it 'Sappho,' with two." The result was that Mr. Daudet cabled back to Messrs. Funk & Wagnalls, care of *The Voice*, New York, "Spell it with two p's."

The effect on Messrs. Funk & Wagnalls has happily not been recorded. Such apparently is the danger of reflections upon moral questions which involve more than one nationality.

In venturing to speak at such a time to such an audience as this, I am reminded of the old saying, "Who shall speak after the king?" We have all been transported by the eloquent words we have listened to, and I am sure we have all been made to feel that he is indeed daft who dares not only to speak after the king, but after the "czar." He is not, it is true, one of the boys of this College, but what we have heard from him further proves what we have long known. He knows his "three R's": he is always *ready*, *resolute*, and *right*. And I, as a Presbyterian elder, am prepared to give him my benediction on what he has said this evening.

What a splendid inspiration it is for us to speak one with another of this College, and what it has done and what it represents! It awakens in us a sharper realization of the fact, that from far beyond the seas men reared under such different intellectual conditions, under such different moral aspirations, and under such different religious teachings, have come to this country and lighted here lamps for the illumination of this new world. How often have I rejoiced, in the days that I have been permitted to preside over our lovely college, amid the hills that overlook the upper Delaware, to think of the young man who, fired with the love of liberty, left home, family, country,—everything that was dear to him,—and came to this people who were as yet not a nation, and who had but a little land upon the border of an unexplored forest and set upon the margin of a mighty sea! With prophetic instinct he

looked beyond the years that were and beheld, as we have
been told that Stephen Girard saw, the years that were
about to be. How great was the heritage which he per-
ceived that not only this people, but the universal hosts
of liberty were about to enter into in America! Think of
him and of his devotion to this country; of how he went
back and tried to reason with "that rabble devil-born," as
they raved in the streets of Paris, mistaking the outcry of
mad social discontent for the glorious voice of liberty;
think how he suffered, how he was imprisoned, how he
endured everything, and never once permitted himself to
desecrate the principles of freedom as he had been taught
them in this country by Washington and his glorious com-
rades! What a wonderful thing it is to think that we, in
this day, have built a college in the midst of a Pennsyl-
vania-German population, under the control of a Scotch-
Irish *clientèle*, and dedicated to the name of a Frenchman!
It seems incongruous, no doubt. But, after all, it is true
that here under the great pavilion that has been spread
in the name of Liberty, practising that pure morality which
was so dear to Stephen Girard,.we are gathering together
the children of all the nations of the earth, and men like
Stephen Girard are providing for them an education, and
a training in right principles, that they may all grow up to
be free men and true Americans. It is sweet to tell the
tale of liberty, and to count its heroes from the first who
came to these shores. Many of them have received but
little recognition for what they were and what they
wrought. It was with peculiar delight that I read, in the
last few days, the splendid defence which Professor John
Fiske, from his study in Boston, has made of doughty Captain John Smith, one of the beginners of the story of free-

dom in America. I love to recount that story, taking
within the compass of my thoughts not only the Cavalier
of Virginia and the Puritan of Massachusetts, but also the
Huguenot of Long Island and the Hollander of Man-
hattan, the Friend of Pennsylvania and the German of
Germantown (not even forgetting Bucks County), the
Scotch-Irish of the Cumberland Valley and the Scotch of
North Carolina. Every one of these nationalities, whatever they may have been, are all parts of the great American people. God bless them all! Each has contributed
men of mark, whether they were of that class that came
already blessed with something good and gracious, or of
that to which Abraham Lincoln belonged, who came out
of the silent squalor of the mountains of Kentucky, and
wandered through the swamp-lands of the Indiana and
Illinois of early days, and thence down the Mississippi on
its flat-boats, learning with painful industry the way of
knowledge, that he might tread the path of righteousness.
When we think of what such men have accomplished for
themselves; when we think of the pain, the agony, the
self-denial of the struggle which they had to undergo;
when we think of how Lincoln and his fellows rose and
stood face to face with intrenched falsehood, and mastered
it in its intrenchments, is it any wonder that we rejoice
that colleges like this have been founded by the munificence of men like Stephen Girard, that they may point not
only hundreds but thousands, every year, along the way
that is most certain and sure to useful citizenship in this
great Commonwealth of Pennsylvania? Oh, that such an
institution might be imitated in the other States! Oh,
that Pennsylvania might make more of Girard College!

The work that is being done here is too little known and recognized.

I remember very well that, when a little boy, I found in a scrap-book a picture of Stephen Girard and of this beautiful first building. The building so impressed itself on my mind that I have never forgotten it. It has always stood out before me as the very ideal of a college; and in my happy college days, when I was a student in one of the universities on the other side of the ocean, to which reference has been made this evening, not even Oxford, with its lovely monuments of Gothic architecture, ever seemed more beautiful than this first building here. How little we appreciate the importance of such a building as a centre of association in the mind of youth and as a formative ideal! When at home I look out from our fair hill upon the mountains around about, upon the river flowing seaward, upon the clouds sailing through the blue heavens, which bend above the purple hills, and I think that surely such associations must uplift our boys, even as the scenes in the hill country of Judæa uplifted the heart of David, to a serene walk with God. How wonderful such associations are! What an undying influence the mere communion with yonder building must create!

Again, how wise was Mr. Girard's provision for instruction in the principles of a pure patriotism! I can remember, as I can remember nothing else from those days, when it was a question whether Kentucky was a State of the Union or not, when John Morgan and his rough riders again and again rode through the streets of our little city, how my mother, with most strenuous intensity of feeling, taught me to love *our* flag. There were few, in the Reconstruction days that followed, who really clung with

unfaltering affection to that dear old flag. I was only a
child at the time, but under such teaching my affection for
the Stars and Stripes grew deep and strong. With what
a thrill of joy, in later years, have I seen unexpectedly in
the ports of Europe that emblem of liberty! Surely our
hearts should feel a thrill of gladness for what America is;
for what men like Stephen Girard have done their part to
make it; for that yet nobler, higher, dearer thing which it
is the privilege and the possibility of this generation to
make it in the interest of peace and prosperity, of the welfare of men and the service of God.

Up yonder on that hill at home, where there was once
a monument to one of the benefactors of Pennsylvania,
there is now a blackened ruin. How my heart sinks every
time I go by it, and I think again of that day, just two
weeks ago, when that beautiful building went up in flames!
But I never pass it by that I do not say to myself, "Look
forward and not back, look up and not down." And
surely that is the motto for America. We can make of
these institutions, as has been made of this College, a
wonderful power for good. It is a thing for us all to be
proud of that the management of this Institution has fallen
into such good hands, and that the direction of the youth
within its walls is in such excellent keeping. I am sure
we all rejoice with President Fetterolf and the representatives of the City Trusts of Philadelphia in the work that
we see, and that we know is going farther forward unto
perfection.

ADDRESS

BY THEODORE L. DEBOW, '57.

Mr. President, Ladies and Gentlemen:—I am deeply sensible of the honor conferred upon me in representing on this interesting occasion the first one hundred boys who entered this Institution fifty years ago. Time has made sad inroads in our members, there being but a fraction of the original hundred left, and of the officers and teachers not one remains who gathered with us at the inaugural services on the first day of January, 1848. Time has also made great changes in the Institution itself; not, however, bringing to it decrepitude and decay with its fifty years of existence, but, like the sturdy oak of the forest, it has gathered increasing strength from year to year, striking its roots deeper into its native soil, spreading its branches far out into the atmosphere about it, and raising its head high into the vaulted blue above, until it seems to have completely filled the whole territory in which it was originally planted, the extent of which, perhaps, Mr. Girard, in his utmost expectations, had supposed it would take many years to grow. The first hundred had a great inheritance of air and sky, of fields and woods that seemed almost boundless.

> No pent-up Utica constrained our powers,
> For the whole boundless universe was ours.

99

Now we see a multiplicity of stately buildings, beautiful in their architecture, teeming with activity and usefulness, spreading over the whole landscape. The fields and the woods, that to our childish hearts were so dear, have given place to the honest and lusty growth of development during the first half-century of our history, so that we cry out in our amazement, " Whereunto will this thing grow?"

When the first hundred took possession of this vast estate, we knew that others after a while would come to share it with us, and so we welcomed the second hundred and made room for them, sharing our bounties with them, even though we thought we had a little less of the air and the fields and the woods than we had before, but when the third hundred were introduced, we felt positively crowded and the College seemed no longer what it was. One thing, however, we were willing that they all should share even down to the last generation of the new-comers, viz., the lessons, the discipline and the rod.

None can know without its experience the loneliness of a boy bereft of his father; none but the Infinite eye witnessed the tears shed on many a narrow bed as the boy, separated from all he loved, entered upon his life in Girard College. But Stephen Girard knew what it was to be lonely, to be friendless, and it may be in the quiet hours of the night shed honest tears in the memory of his boyhood, and being childless, he yearned to gather to his empty heart and fireside the fatherless boys of his adopted city. And so he kept trading, and saving, and planning with this growing, burning hope in his heart, until it became all-absorbing, producing the magnificent results of which we have only seen the first fruits.

A boy's life in Girard College is about the same now as

it was fifty years ago, and there is not much that can be
said, except, perhaps, that the boys inside have, on the
whole, a very much better time than the boys on the outside, and the first hundred thought they had the better of
all that came after. As I look back over the years, I am
impressed with this fact, that the boy that has devoted a
fair share of time and attention to his opportunities here,
is sent forth into the world with a mental and moral equipment that challenges comparison, other things being
equal, with any institution in the land. I am well satisfied
from observation that the studious Girard College boy
has a better outlook for earning his living and battling for
a successful career than a very large percentage of rich
men's sons. The advantage I claim is, that the education
here makes us practical men, and throughout this great
city and State several thousand men, former boys of this
College, have achieved success in the various avocations
of life. Without money capital they have risen step by
step, filling places of honor and usefulness in their different communities.

I will not enumerate the professions, or lines of business, which many of our brothers are filling with great
success, nor mention the names of those whose success is
our pride, but, for the information of our distinguished
guest, I will say that two of them had the honor to be
members of Congress but a few years ago,—one from the
Chester district of this State, and one from the Petersburg
district of Virginia, and both of them were Republicans.

The mental training of the boys has been, and is now
certainly, of the very best, and the teachers and professors,
they were of the very best, too. Many of the latter have
gone to their reward, but their memory is precious to us

7

that remain. Concerning the moral training, it used to be said that Girard College was atheistic, or that Mr. Girard was an infidel, so that many a poor mother has been afraid to bring her sons here, because she was told that the fear of God was not taught. I think these lies have been buried so long that they can never be resurrected. Can we ever forget the many instructive lessons from the desk on Sundays, and the sweet hymns taught by Kingsley, Bird, Fisher and others; of the morning and evening prayers, and the Scriptures with the unpronounceable names, and the stories of the battles of Israel with the Moabites, the Jebusites, Hittites, etc., etc.? Who will ever forget the many delightful and profitable Sunday afternoons with Judge Kelley in his prime, or René Guillou, Joseph R. Chandler, William Welsh, President Allen, and others? Ladies and gentlemen, I am ready to acknowledge that under the instructions of the Sabbath-day, many a time I felt that I was mean and wicked, and many a time I promised God on my knees that I would be a better boy.

The love of country was instilled in our young minds by American history and the example of our noble benefactor. No wonder, then, that, when the Civil War broke out, hundreds of our boys sprang to arms at the call of the government; many laid down their lives, and sleep to-night with the honored dead. Yonder monument erected to their memory is a living testimonial of the patriotic instructions received here as boys, bearing fruit in our lives as men. Some of the first hundred's names are inscribed on the tablets there.

Oh, these crowding memories of our boyhood days, how delightful they are! Standing upon the threshold of a new half-century, and in this presence, I fancy I see a face and form of one who has long since gone to rest. In form he was massive, with broad intellectual brow and kindly blue eyes. He was kind yet firm, deeply learned yet simple. He gave the best years of his life to the development of our youth, and he now sleeps the sleep of the Just. Such was President Allen. We esteem him a great man, and no wonder, for he came originally from the State where great men are raised, the State of Maine.

Another form appears to my view, one who stood with us here fifty years ago. In the vigor of a strong intellect and a mature womanhood she began the duties of a teacher. So well were these duties discharged that she was asked to assume more important ones. Stern in appearance and word, but conscientious in matters of duty, compelling obedience from all, superintending our comforts by day, and watching by the beds of the sick at night; childless yet the mother of hundreds. And when the boys went from here to make a start in the world she packed each trunk with her own hands, into each of which she put a copy of the Scriptures and a prayer. She spent her life willingly in this work, and fell asleep in full view of the scenes of her labor. Such was the Matron Jane Mitchell.

One other form appears on this scene. She, too, was here fifty years ago. A teacher of the younger boys. Fair of face and form, faithful and devoted. Her countenance reflected the purity of her soul. She lived her whole life, from that time until her translation a few months ago, in the ministry of love and a conscientious, faithful discharge of duty. I refer to Mary Lynch.

I stood this evening in the presence of two aged men whose labors here have been almost coextensive with the history of the College; their instruction touching almost, if not all, the boys from the beginning until the present; but now their labors are nearly ended; the time of their departure is at hand; they have fought a good fight; they have finished their course; henceforth there is laid up for them a crown. We stand before them with heads uncovered as we look upon their venerable forms. God bless these veteran professors, George J. Becker and Warren Holden.

I do not name these in invidious distinction, for others also could be named whose memories are like "ointment poured forth." These have their succesors, equally worthy, but we leave for them a tribute from others fifty years hence.

I may be pardoned if I speak a word concerning the management by the Directors of the Board of City Trusts. Many of the honorable men who have held these positions are gone to their reward, who share the happiness of this occasion in spirit perhaps, among whom we remember Joseph R. Chandler, William Cowperthwait, William Biddle, Mordecai L. Dawson, Judge Campbell, William B. Mann, and others whose names I do not now recall. These men, their colleagues and successors are to be held in everlasting remembrance for fidelity to their trust, for the faithful execution of the plans, purposes and will of Mr. Girard. How well these interests have been preserved is evidenced by our surroundings, and while others have spoken eloquently from without, we from within would utter a hearty indorsement of it all.

Gentlemen of the Board of City Trusts, we extend to you our heartfelt thanks for your unselfish and untiring devotion to these great interests, and we hope in the future, as in the past, the Board will always be constituted

of the very best men our city affords.   Men of clean hands
and pure hearts.   May you each at the end receive the
plaudit of the King, " Well done, thou good and faithful
servant."

Brothers, when the Centennial Anniversary of this Institution is observed most of us shall have joined the great
majority, until that time let us be true to the memory of
Stephen Girard, true to ourselves, and true to God.

APPENDIX

STEPHEN GIRARD STATUE, CITY HALL PLAZA.

STEPHEN GIRARD—MARINER AND MERCHANT

A BIOGRAPHICAL SKETCH

BY GEORGE P. RUPP,

Librarian of Girard College.

Stephen Girard was born on the 20th of May, 1750, in the Rue Ramonet aux Chartrons, a suburb of the city of Bordeaux, France. He was the eldest son and the second child of Captain Pierre Girard. When eight years old he met with an accident by which the sight of his right eye was destroyed. This personal defect and the ridicule it occasioned no doubt had its effect upon his character. The men of the Girard family generally followed the sea for a living, and, without doubt, Stephen Girard inherited a like inclination.

When not quite fourteen years old, he, with his father's consent, sailed in a vessel, the "Pèlerin," for San Domingo. From 1764 to 1773 he traded between Bordeaux and the West Indies, attaining the rank of lieutenant of the vessel. Mr. Girard had now become a skilful navigator, and he had made up for some of the defects of his early education by study and observation. In October, 1773, he was granted a license to act as captain of a vessel. In the ship "La Julie" he left Bordeaux for San Domingo, reaching there in February, 1774. Having disposed of the cargo, he sailed for New York, and landed there in July,

1774, this being his first visit to the United States. The ability he displayed in the business of disposing of the cargo he brought in the "La Julie," attracted the notice of Mr. Thomas Randall, a merchant of New York, and his assistance enabled Mr. Girard to trade successfully between New York, New Orleans, and Port au Prince.

While acting jointly with Mr. Randall, as part owner of the vessel called "L'aimable Louise," Mr. Girard was returning from the West Indies, when he was forced, by the presence of a British fleet, to enter Delaware Bay, and he arrived for the first time in Philadelphia in May, 1776. On account of the war of the Revolution, the port of Philadelphia was blockaded by the British, and, knowing the danger to American ships, he sold his interest in "L'aimable Louise" and opened a store on Water Street. From this time Mr. Girard could no longer be considered a mariner, though he continued in the shipping business.

In the north-eastern section of Philadelphia there was a ship-builder named Lum, whom Mr. Girard consulted about the building of a new vessel. While on this business he met Mary Lum, or "Polly" as she was familiarly called, a girl about sixteen years old, distinguished for her personal beauty and her noble virtues. After a brief courtship they were married by the Rev. Mr. Stringer, in St. Paul's Episcopal Church, on the 6th of June, 1777. On the approach of the British army to take possession of Philadelphia, Mr. Girard, with his wife, left for Mount Holly, having purchased a small farm there from a Mr. Hazlehurst, who had at one time been his partner.

In October, 1778, two years after his arrival in Philadelphia, Mr. Girard took the oath of allegiance to the State of Pennsylvania. On his return to Philadelphia from

Mount Holly, he resumed his business, directing his attention especially to the West India trade. His previous experience, combined with unflagging labor and economy, greatly aided in making his progress to fortune rapid and, at the same time, sure. His father-in-law, Mr. Lum, built for him a sloop, the "Water-Witch," and, as it was through the planning of this boat that he had met his wife, he naturally regarded it with affection, and had a superstition that it could never cause him loss.

Mr. Girard pursued so successfully the New Orleans and West India trade, and his gains increased to such an extent, that he was able to greatly extend his enterprises. In 1780 he entered into partnership with his brother Jean, but contentions arose, and these became so bitter that the partnership was soon dissolved.

About this time Mrs. Girard fell into a state of melancholy, which became so pronounced that, after a consultation with prominent physicians, Mr. Girard reluctantly consented to place her in the Pennsylvania Hospital. Shortly after she had been admitted she gave birth to a child, which was baptized Mary, but which died in a few months. Mrs. Girard remained an inmate of the hospital for twenty-five years, and died there on September 15, 1815.

In 1791, Mr. Girard commenced building those fine ships which were, in their day, the pride of Philadelphia, and which soon engaged in trade with the most important seaports of the world. They were named the "Rousseau," "Voltaire," "Montesquieu," "Helvétius;" and these names show that he had an affectionate regard for the philosophers of his native land.

In 1790, the Bank of the United States was established by an act of Congress. It received a charter which limited

its existence to twenty years. With its capital of ten millions of dollars it was a powerful agency in establishing the
credit of the government, in facilitating its financial operations, and in promoting its industry and commerce. The
bank began business in Carpenters' Hall in Philadelphia,.
with branches in other cities. In 1797 it was removed to
the new building on Third Street below Chestnut Street.

In 1810, Mr. Girard had about a million dollars with the
house of Baring Bros. & Co., of London. Owing to the
Barings being on the verge of bankruptcy, Mr. Girard's
money was in peril. He succeeded in obtaining his funds
by the purchase of British goods, and of shares in the Bank
of the United States. The act of Congress to recharter the
bank having been defeated, the bank closed, and Mr. Girard purchased the bank building and cashier's house for
one-third their original cost, and on the 12th of May, 1812,
he opened the Bank of Stephen Girard.

When, in 1814, the resources of the country were at
the lowest ebb, the treasury bankrupt, a foreign foe marching through the land, and when under these conditions the
government asked for a loan of five millions of dollars, and
the inducement of a large bonus, and interest at seven per
cent., with the result that only twenty thousand dollars
of the amount asked for was subscribed, then Mr. Girard
came forward and subscribed for the large balance of over
four and a half millions of dollars. This act of patriotism
restored public confidence, and those who had refused to
subscribe were now willing to pay an advance; but Mr.
Girard would not take advantage of these offers, and al-
lowed them to purchase on the same terms. The sinews
of war having been furnished, a series of brilliant victories
followed and peace was restored.

In 1793, Philadelphia was visited by an epidemic of yellow fever, and a reign of terror, suffering, and desolation prevailed throughout the city. The people became panic-stricken, and the roads leading from the city were crowded with fugitives. Hundreds of houses became tenantless, and the hearse was the vehicle most frequently seen. Self-preservation made the people forget the commonest instincts of humanity.

In response to an advertisement in the *Federal Gazette,* on the 12th of September, 1793, twenty-seven noble-hearted men met at the City Hall to take measures to relieve the distress. Attention was first paid to the hospital at Bush Hill, which was reported as being "without order or arrangement, and far from being clean." To enter this pest-house was thought to be a passage to the grave. At one of the meetings of this committee an incident occurred which is best to give in the words of the late Matthew Carey:

"At the meeting on the 15th, a circumstance [occurred] to which the most glowing pencil can hardly do justice. Stephen Girard, a wealthy merchant, a native of France, and one of the members of the committee, touched with the wretched condition of the sufferers at Bush Hill, voluntarily and unexpectedly offered himself as a manager to superintend that hospital. The surprise and satisfaction, excited by this extraordinary effort of humanity, can be better conceived than expressed. Peter Helm, a native of Pennsylvania, also a member, offered his services in the same department. Their offers were accepted ; and the same afternoon they entered on the execution of their dangerous and praiseworthy office.

"To form a just estimate of the value of the offer of these men, it is necessary to take in full consideration the general consternation which at that period pervaded every quarter of the city, and which made attendance on the sick be regarded as a little less than a certain sacrifice. Uninfluenced by any reflections of this kind, without any possible inducement but the purest motives of humanity, they came forward and offered themselves as the forlorn hope of the committee. I trust that the gratitude of their fellow-citizens will remain as long as the memory of their beneficent conduct, which I hope will not die with the present generation."

Mr. Girard immediately took charge of the interior of the hospital, and he soon made his wonderful influence felt. Order reigned where all had been chaos, cleanliness where filth had been supreme; and within twenty-four hours he reported the hospital ready to afford every assistance. As one turns over the pages of the minutes of the committee, day after day, for nearly two months, we find the line, "Stephen Girard and Peter Helm at the hospital." Nor did the services of that committee end when the disease ceased to exist. They supplied the poor with money, provisions, and fuel. They furnished burial for the dead. They took under their care one hundred and ninety-two orphans of those who had died of the fever, and they only ceased their labors when they had taken precautions against a similar calamity in the future. We can form some idea of the terrible results of this epidemic, from the fact that from the 1st of August to the 9th of November, 1793, there were four thousand and thirty deaths, nearly one-tenth of the population.

Mr. Girard placed a very modest estimate upon his services during this period. Yet few men have equalled him in the courage and spirit of humanity he displayed.

In 1802, Mr. Girard was elected by his fellow-citizens to the Councils of the city of Philadelphia, and he was a faithful and useful member for several terms. For over twenty-two years he was also a member of the Board of Wardens of the port of Philadelphia. Mr. Girard's public spirit was again manifested when he subscribed one hundred and ten thousand dollars for the improvement of the navigation of the Schuylkill River, and the subscription and the temporary loans which he made to the Chesapeake and Delaware Canal.   When, also, the Commonwealth of Pennsylvania, in 1829, found its treasury empty, it was Mr. Girard who loaned one hundred thousand dollars, affording the Commonwealth the relief it so badly needed.   This was probably the last public act of Mr. Girard's life, for his long career of unceasing toil was drawing to a close.   Refusing assistance from others, he insisted on giving the same careful attention to the details of his great business, and daily walked from his residence on Water Street to his banking-house on Third Street.   On February 12, 1830, while crossing the street, at Second and Market Streets, he was struck and seriously injured by a rapidly driven wagon. His health now declined, and an attack of influenza, then prevalent in Philadelphia, prostrated him, and he died on December 26, 1831, at four o'clock in the afternoon, aged eighty-one years, seven months, and six days, after a life of labor, perseverance, economy, and success which has rarely been equalled.

When his death became known, there was a universal expression of sorrow at the decease of such a distinguished citizen.   At a meeting of the authorities of the city, it was decided to give him a civic funeral; the flags of the shipping and public buildings were displayed at half-mast; the Councils of the city adopted resolutions of regret, and their respective halls were draped in mourning.   The funeral, which was attended by a large number of citizens and all the public authorities, took place on December 30, 1831, and the mortal remains of the honored "Mariner and Merchant" were taken to the Holy Trinity Roman Catholic

Church and placed in a vault belonging to the Baron Lallemand. After nearly twenty years his remains were removed and placed in a marble sarcophagus in the vestibule of Girard College.

A full knowledge of Stephen Girard's character conveys, in the minds of those who have studied it, a vivid impression of his remarkable qualities. He was not tall, but of very solid build, with a short, thick neck and fearless temperament, all his sturdy endowments took the direction of indomitable energy in enterprise and of intrepid assertion in everything right and good.

Let it be granted that he was eccentric, but eccentricity needs defining. He was a rare example of a life where a man's word was as good as his bond. Money, however, was not his God. He did not accumulate property for the mere love of it. He believed that the true blessings of life came through justice and not mercy.

Two facts stand out prominently in the earthly passage of this markedly gifted man,—his devotion to his fellowmen and his love for his adopted country. He was fearless, because he was a strong man, whose hope dimmed not, whose faith faltered not, and whose courage forsook him not. By residence he belonged to Philadelphia, by faith to the Roman Catholic Church; but in a truer, wider sense he belonged to no city, to no sect, but to the people, to the cause of the greatest good for all men. Whatever he espoused, whatever he touched, he enriched with the genius of a determined spirit strong for success.

Poor, struggling, full of ambition, full of hope in his youth; active, determined, enterprising, and charitable in the prime of life; mourned and regretted in his death; such was the life of the most eminent philanthropist of his time, who lies in the beautiful Greek temple he planned, awaiting the day when all shall be judged.

To write Mr. Girard's life means to write the financial and commercial history of the city and country during its early and critical periods.

WILL OF STEPHEN GIRARD

Dated February 16, 1830.   *Codicils, dated December* 25, 1830,
and June 20, 1831.

Proved December 31, 1831.

Recorded Philada. Will Book 10, *p.* 198.

I, Stephen Girard, of the City of Philadelphia, in the
Commonwealth of Pennsylvania, mariner and merchant,
being of sound mind, memory, and understanding, do
make and publish this my last will and testament, in manner following, that is to say. . . .

I.   I give and bequeath unto " The Contributors to the
Pennsylvania Hospital," of which corporation I am a
member, the sum of *thirty thousand dollars,* upon the following conditions, namely, that the said sum shall be added
to their capital, and shall remain a part thereof forever, to
be placed at interest and the interest thereof to be applied,
in the first place to pay to my black woman Hannah (to
whom I hereby give her freedom) the sum of two hundred
dollars per year, in quarterly payments of fifty dollars each
in advance, during all the term of her life; and, *in the
second place,* the said interest to be applied to the use and
accommodation of the sick in the said hospital, and for
providing and at all times having competent matrons, and
a sufficient number of nurses and assistant nurses, in order
not only to promote the purposes of the said hospital, but

118

to encrease this last class of useful persons much wanted in our city:

II.   I give and bequeath to "The Pennsylvania Institution for the Deaf and Dumb" the sum of *twenty thousand dollars*, for the use of that institution:

III.   I give and bequeath to "the Orphan Asylum of Philadelphia" the sum of *ten thousand dollars* for the use of that Institution:

IV.   I give and bequeath to "the Comptrollers of the public schools for the city and county of Philadelphia" the sum of *ten thousand dollars* for the use of the schools upon the Lancaster system, in the first section of the first school district of Pennsylvania.

V.   I give and bequeath to "The Mayor, Aldermen and Citizens of Philadelphia," the sum of *ten thousand dollars*, in trust safely to invest the same in some productive fund, and with the interest and dividends arising therefrom to purchase fuel between the months of March and August in every year forever, and in the month of January in every year forever distribute the same, amongst poor white house-keepers and room-keepers, of good character, residing in the city of Philadelphia.

VI.   I give and bequeath to the society for the relief of poor and distressed masters of ships, their widows and children, (of which society I am a member) the sum of ten thousand dollars to be added to their capital stock, for the uses and purposes of said society:

VII.   I give and bequeath to the gentlemen, who shall be trustees of the Masonic Loan at the time of my decease, the sum of *twenty thousand dollars*, including therein ten thousand and nine hundred dollars due to me, part of the Masonic Loan, and any interest that may be due thereon at the time of my decease, in trust for the use and benefit of "the Grand Lodge of Pennsylvania and masonic jurisdiction thereto belonging," and to be paid over by the said trustees to the said Grand Lodge for the purposes of being invested in some safe stock or funds, or other good security, and the dividends and interest arising therefrom to be again so invested and added to the capital, without applying any part thereof to any other purpose until the whole capital shall amount to thirty thousand dollars, when the same shall forever after remain a permanent fund or capital, of the said amount of thirty thousand dollars, the interest whereof shall be applied from time to time to the relief of poor and respectable brethren: and in order that the real and benevolent purposes of masonic institutions may be attained, I recommend to the several lodges not to admit to membership, or to receive members from other lodges, unless the applicants shall absolutely be men of sound and good morals.

VIII. I give and bequeath unto Philip Peltz, John Lentz, Francis Hesley, Jacob Baker and Adam Young, of Passyunk township, in the county of Philadelphia, the sum of *six thousand dollars*, in trust that they or the survivors or survivor of them shall purchase a suitable piece of ground, as near as may be in the centre of said township, and thereon erect a substantial brick building, sufficiently large for a school house and the residence of a school-master, one part thereof for poor male white children, and the other part for poor female white children of said township: and as soon as the said school-house shall have been built, that they the said trustees or the survivors or survivor of them shall convey the said piece of ground and house thereon erected, and shall pay over such balance of said sum as may remain unexpended, to any board of directors and their successors in trust, which may at the time exist or be by law constituted, consisting of at least twelve discreet inhabitants of the said township, and to be annually chosen by the inhabitants thereof; the said piece of ground and house to be carefully maintained by said directors and their successors solely for the purposes of a school as aforesaid forever, and the said balance to be securely invested as a permanent fund, the interest thereof to be applied from time to time towards the education in the said school of any number of such poor white children of said township; and I do hereby recommend to the citizens of the said township to make additions to the fund whereof I have laid the foundation.

IX. I give and devise my house and lot of ground thereto belonging, situate in rue Ramonet aux Chartrons, near the city of Bordeaux, in France, and the rents issues and profits thereof to my brother Etienne Girard and my niece Victoire Fenellon (daughter of my late sister Sophia Girard Capayron) (both residing in France) in equal moieties for the life of my said brother, and, on his decease, one moiety of the said house and lot to my said niece Victoire and her heirs forever, and the other moiety to the six children of my said brother, namely John Fabricius, Marguerite, Anne Henriette, Jean August, Marie, and Madelaine Henriette, share and share alike (the issue of any deceased child if more than one to take amongst them the parent's share) and their heirs forever.

X. I give and bequeath to my said brother Etienne Girard the sum of *five thousand dollars,* and the like sum of *five thousand dollars* to each of his six children above named: if any of the said children shall die prior to the receipt of his or her legacy of five thousand dollars, the said sum shall be paid, and I give and bequeath the same, to any issue of such deceased child, if more than one share and share alike.

XI. I give and bequeath to my said niece Victoire Fenellon the sum of *five thousand dollars.*

XII. I give and bequeath absolutely to my niece Antoinetta, now married to Mr Hemphill, the sum of *ten thousand dollars,* and I also give and bequeath to her the sum of *fifty thousand dollars,* to be paid over to a trustee or trustees to be appointed by my executors, which trustee or trustees shall place and continue the said sum of fifty thousand dollars upon good security, and pay the interest and dividends thereof as they shall from time to time accrue, to my said niece for her separate use, during the term of her life, and from and immediately after her decease, to pay and distribute the capital to and among such of her children and the issue of deceased children, and in such parts and shares as she the said Antoinetta, by any instrument under her hand and seal executed in the presence of at least two credible witnesses shall direct and appoint, and for default of such appointment then to and among the said children and issue of deceased children in equal shares, such issue of deceased children if more than one to take only the share which their deceased parent would have taken if living.

XIII. I give and bequeath unto my niece Carolina, now married to Mr Haslam, the sum of *ten thousand dollars,* to be paid over to a trustee or trustees to be appointed by my executors, which trustee or trustees shall place and continue the said money upon good security, and pay the interest and dividends thereof from time to time, as they

shall accrue, to my said niece, for her separate use during
the term of her life; and, from and immediately after her
decease, to pay and distribute the capital to and among
such of her children and issue of deceased children, and
in such parts and shares, as she the said Carolina, by any
instrument under her hand and seal executed, in the presence of at least two credible witnesses, shall direct and
appoint, and for default of such appointment, then to and
among the said children and issue of deceased children, in
equal shares, such issue of deceased children if more than
one, to take only the share which the deceased parent
would have taken if living: but if my said niece Carolina
shall leave no issue, then the said trustee or trustees on
her decease shall pay the said capital and any interest accrued thereon to and among Caroline Lallemand (niece of
the said Carolina) and the children of the aforesaid Antoinetta Hemphill, share and share alike.

XIV.   I give and bequeath to my niece Henrietta, now
married to Dr Clark, the sum of *ten thousand dollars;* and
I give and bequeath to her daughter Caroline (in the last
clause above named) the sum of twenty thousand dollars
—the interest of the said sum of twenty thousand dollars,
or so much thereof as may be necessary, to be applied to
the maintenance and education of the said Caroline during
her minority, and the principal with any accumulated interest to be paid to the said Caroline, on her arrival at the
age of twenty-one years.

XV.   Unto each of the captains, who shall be in my
employment at the time of my decease, either in port or
at sea, having charge of one of my ships or vessels, and
having performed at least two voyages in my service, I
give and bequeath the sum of *fifteen hundred dollars—*

provided he shall have brought safely into the port of Philadelphia, or if at sea at the time of my decease shall bring safely into that port, my ship or vessel last entrusted to him, and also that his conduct during the last voyage shall have been in every respect conformable to my instructions to him.

XVI.   All persons, who, at the time of my decease, shall be bound to me by indenture, as apprentices or servants, and who shall then be under age, I direct my executors to assign to suitable masters immediately after my decease, for the remainder of their respective terms, on conditions as favorable as they can in regard to education, clothing, and freedom dues; to each of the said persons, in my service and under age at the time of my decease I give and bequeath the sum of *five hundred dollars*, which sums respectively I direct my executors safely to invest in public stock, to apply the interest and dividends thereof towards the education of the several apprentices or servants, for whom the capital is given, respectively, and at the termination of the apprenticeship or service of each to pay to him or her the said sum of five hundred dollars and any interest accrued thereon, if any such interest shall remain unexpended: in assigning any indenture, preference shall be given to the mother, father, or next relation, as assignee, should such mother, father, or relative desire it, and be at the same time respectable and competent.

XVII.   I give and bequeath to Francis Hesley (son of Mʳ S. Hesley, who is mother of Marianne Hesley) the sum of *one thousand dollars*, over and above such sum as may be due to him at my decease.

XVIII.   I charge my real estate in the state of Pennsylvania with the payment of the several annuities or sums following (the said annuities to be paid by the treasurer or other proper officer of the city of Philadelphia appointed by the corporation thereof for the purpose out of the **rents and profits** of said **real estate**, hereinafter directed to be kept **constantly rented**) **namely:**

1. I give and bequeath to Mrs Elizabeth Ingersoll, widow of Jared Ingersoll, esq. late of the city of Philadelphia, counsellor at law, an annuity or yearly sum of *one thousand dollars*, to be paid in half yearly payments, in advance, of five hundred dollars each during her life:—

2. I give and bequeath to Mrs Catherine Girard, now widow of Mr J. B. Hoskins, who died in the isle of France, an annuity or yearly sum of *four hundred dollars*, to be paid in half yearly payments in advance of two hundred dollars each, during her life.

3. I give and bequeath to Mrs Jane Taylor, my present house keeper (the widow of the late captain Alexander Taylor, who was master of my ship Helvetius and died in my employment) an annuity or yearly sum of *five hundred dollars*, to be paid in half yearly payments in advance of two hundred and fifty dollars each, during her life.

4. I give and bequeath to Mrs S. Hesley, my house-keeper at my place in Passyunk Township, an annuity or yearly sum of *five hundred dollars*, to be paid in half yearly payments in advance of two hundred and fifty dollars each during her life.

5. I give and bequeath to Marianne Hesley, daughter of Mrs S. Hesley, an annuity or yearly sum of *three hundred dollars*, to be paid to her mother for her use in half yearly payments in advance of one hundred and fifty dollars each, until the said Marianne shall have attained the age of twenty-one years, when the said annuity shall cease, and

the said Marianne will receive the five hundred dollars given to her and other indented persons, according to clause XVI. of this will:

6. I give and bequeath to my late house-keeper, Mary Kenton, an annuity or yearly sum of *three hundred dollars* to be paid in half yearly payments in advance of one hundred and fifty dollars each during her life.

7. I give and bequeath to Mrs Deborah Scott, sister of Mary Kenton, and wife of Mr Edwin T. Scott, an annuity or yearly sum of *three hundred dollars*, to be paid in half yearly payments in advance of one hundred and fifty dollars each, during her life.

8. I give and bequeath to Mrs Catharine McLaren, sister of Mary Kenton, and wife of Mr M. McLaren, an annuity or yearly sum of *three hundred dollars*, to be paid in half yearly payments in advance of one hundred and fifty dollars each, during her life.

9. I give and bequeath to Mrs Amelia G. Taylor, wife of Mr Richd M. Taylor, an annuity or yearly sum of *three hundred dollars* to be paid in half yearly payments in advance of one hundred and fifty dollars each during her life.

XIX. All that part of my real and personal estate, near Washita, in the state of Louisiana, the said real estate consisting of upwards of two hundred and eight thousand arpens or acres of land, and including therein the settlement hereinafter mentioned, I give, devise, and bequeath, as follows, namely: 1. I give devise and bequeath to the corporation of the City of New Orleans, their successors and assigns, all that part of my real estate, constituting the settlement formed on my behalf by my particular friend Judge Henry Bree, of Washita, consisting of upwards of one thousand arpens or acres of land with the appurte-

nances and improvements thereon, and also all the personal
estate thereto belonging and thereon remaining, including
upwards of thirty slaves now on said settlement and their
encrease, in trust, however, and subject to the following
reservations: I desire, that no part of the said estate or
property, or the slaves thereon, or their encrease, shall be
disposed of or sold for the term of twenty years from and
after my decease, should the said judge Henry Bree sur-
vive me and live so long, but that the said settlement shall
be kept up by the said judge Henry Bree, for and during
said term of twenty years, as if it was his own, that is, it
shall remain under his sole care and control, he shall improve the same by raising such produce as he may deem
most advisable, and, after paying taxes, and all expenses
in keeping up the settlement by clothing the slaves and
otherwise, he shall have and enjoy for his own use all the
nett profits of said settlement:—provided however and I
desire that the said judge Henry Bree shall render annually
to the corporation of the City of New Orleans, a report
of the state of the settlement, the income and expenditure
thereof, the number and encrease of the slaves, and the
nett result of the whole. I desire that, at the expiration
of the said term of twenty years, or on the decease of the
said Judge Henry Bree, should he not live so long, the
land and improvements forming said settlement, the slaves
thereon or thereto belonging, and all other appurtenant
personal property, shall be sold, as soon as the said Corporation shall deem it advisable to do so, and the proceeds
of the said sale or sales shall be applied by the said corporation to such uses and purposes as they shall consider
most likely to promote the health and general prosperity
of the inhabitants of the city of New Orleans: But, until

the said sale shall be made, the said corporation shall pay all taxes, prevent waste or intrusion, and so manage the said settlement and the slaves and their encrease thereon, as to derive an income, and the said income shall be applied from time to time, to the same uses and purposes for the health and general prosperity of the said inhabitants. 2. I give devise and bequeath to the Mayor Aldermen and citizens of Philadelphia, their successors and assigns, two undivided third parts of all the rest and residue of my said real estate, being the lands unimproved near Washita in the said state of Louisiana, in trust, that, in common with the corporation of the city of New Orleans, they shall pay the taxes on the said lands, and preserve them from waste or intrusion, for the term of ten years from and after my decease, and, at the end of the said term, when they shall deem it advisable to do so, shall sell and dispose of their interest in said lands gradually from time to time, and apply the proceeds of such sales to the same uses and purposes hereinafter declared and directed of and concerning the residue of my personal estate.   3. And I give devise and bequeath to the Corporation of the city of New Orleans, their successors and assigns, the remaining one undivided third part of the said lands, in trust, in common with the Mayor Aldermen and citizens of Philadelphia, to pay the taxes on the said lands and preserve them from waste and intrusion for the term of ten years from and after my decease, and, at the end of the said term when they shall deem it advisable to do so, to sell and dispose of their interest in said lands gradually from time to time, and to apply the proceeds of such sales to such uses and purposes as the said corporation may consider most likely to promote the health and general prosperity of the inhabitants of the City of New Orleans.

XX. And whereas I have been for a long time impressed with the importance of educating the poor, and of placing them by the early cultivation of their minds and the development of their moral principles, above the.many temptations, to which, through poverty and ignorance they are exposed; and I am particularly desirious to provide for such a number of poor male white orphan children, as can be trained in one institution, a better education as well as a more comfortable maintenance than they usually receive from the application of the public funds: And whereas, together with the object just adverted to I have sincerely at heart the welfare of the city of Philadelphia, and, as a part of it, am desirious to improve the neighborhood of the river Delaware, so that the health of the citizens may be promoted and preserved, and that the eastern part of the city may be made to correspond better with the interior: Now, I do give devise and bequeath *all the residue and remainder of my real and personal estate* of every sort and kind and whersoever situate (the real estate in Pennsylvania charged as aforesaid) unto "The Mayor, aldermen and citizens of Philadelphia their successors and assigns in trust to and for the several uses intents and purposes hereinafter mentioned and declared of and concerning the same, that is to say: So far as regards my real estate in Pennsylvania, in trust, that no part thereof shall ever be sold or alienated by the said The Mayor Aldermen and citizens of Philadelphia or their successors, but the same shall forever thereafter be let from time to time to good tenants, at yearly or other rents and upon leases in possession not exceeding five years from the commence-

ment thereof, and that the rents issues and profits arising
therefrom shall be applied towards keeping that part of
the said real estate situate in the city and Liberties of Philadelphia constantly in good repair (parts elsewhere situate
to be kept in repair by the tenants thereof respectively)
and towards improving the same whenever necessary by
erecting new buildings, and that the nett residue (after
paying the several annuities herein before provided for)
be applied to the same uses and purposes as are herein
declared of and concerning the residue of my personal
estate: And so far as regards my real estate in Kentucky,
now under the care of Messrs Triplett and Burmley, in
trust to sell and dispose of the same, whenever it may be
expedient to do so, and to apply the proceeds of such sale
to the same uses and purposes as are herein declared of
and concerning the residue of my personal estate.

XXI.   And so far as regards the residue of my personal
estate, in trust, as to *two millions of dollars*, part thereof,
to apply and expend so much of that sum as may be necessary—in erecting as soon as practicably may be, in the
centre of my square of ground between High and Chestnut
streets and Eleventh and Twelfth streets, in the city of
Philadelphia (which square of ground I hereby devote for
the purposes hereinafter stated, and for no other, forever)
a permanent College, with suitable out-buildings, sufficiently spacious for the residence and accommodation of
at least three hundred scholars, and the requisite teachers
and other persons necessary in such an institution as I
direct to be established; and in supplying the said college
and out-buildings with decent and suitable furniture, as
well as books and all other things needful to carry into
effect my general design. The said College shall be con-

structed with the most durable materials and in the most
permanent manner, avoiding needless ornament, and at-
tending chiefly to the strength, convenience and neatness
of the whole: It shall be at least one hundred and ten
feet east and west, and one hundred and sixty feet north
and south, and shall be built on lines parallel with High
and Chestnut streets and Eleventh and Twelfth streets,
provided those lines shall constitute at their junction right
angles: It shall be three stories in height, each story at
least fifteen feet high in the clear from the floor to the
cornice: it shall be fire-proof inside and outside, the floors
and the roof to be formed of solid materials, on arches
turned on proper centres, so that no wood may be used,
except for doors, windows and shutters: Cellars shall be
made under the whole building, solely for the purposes of
the institution; the doors to them from the outside shall
be on the east and west of the building, and access to them
from the inside shall be had by steps, descending to the
cellar floor from each of the entries or halls hereinafter
mentioned, and the inside cellar doors to open under the
stairs on the north-east and north-west corners of the
northern entry, and under the stairs on the south-east and
south-west corners of the southern entry; there should be
a cellar window under and in a line with, each window in
the first story—they should be built one half below, the
other half above, the surface of the ground, and the ground
outside each window should be supported by stout walls;
the sashes should open inside, on hinges, like doors, and
there should be strong iron bars outside each window; the
windows inside and outside should not be less than four
feet wide in the clear: There shall be in each story four
rooms, each room not less than fifty feet square in the

clear; the four rooms on each floor to occupy the whole space east and west on such floor or story, and the middle of the building north and south; so that in the north of the building, and in the south thereof, there may remain a space of equal dimensions, for an entry or hall in each, for stairs and landings: In the north-east and in the north-west corners of the northern entry or hall on the first floor, stairs shall be made so as to form a double stair-case, which shall be carried up through the several stories; and, in like manner, in the south-east and south-west corners of the southern entry or hall, stairs shall be made, on the first floor, so as to form a double stair-case, to be carried up through the several stories; the steps of the stairs to be made of smooth white marble with plain square edges, each step not to exceed nine inches in the rise, nor to be less than ten inches in the tread: the outside and inside foundation walls shall be at least ten feet high in the clear from the ground to the ceiling: the first floor shall be at least three feet above the level of the ground around the building, after that ground shall have been so regulated as that there shall be a gradual descent from the centre to the sides of the square formed by High and Chestnut and Eleventh and Twelfth streets: all the outside foundation walls, forming the cellars, shall be three feet and six inches thick up to the first floor, or as high as may be necessary to fix the centres for the first floor; and the inside foundation wall, running north and south, and the three inside foundation walls, running east and west, (intended to receive the interior walls for the four rooms each not less than fifty feet square in the clear, above mentioned) shall be three feet thick up to the first floor, or as high as may be necessary to fix the centres for the first floor: when

carried so far up, the outside walls shall be reduced to two
feet in thickness, leaving a recess outside of one foot and
inside of six inches—and when carried so far up, the inside foundation walls shall also be reduced, six inches on
each side, to the thickness of two feet; centres shall then
be fixed on the various recesses of six inches throughout,
left for the purpose, the proper arches shall be turned, and
the first floor laid: the outside and the inside walls shall
then be carried up of the thickness of two feet throughout,
as high as may be necessary to begin the recess intended
to fix the centres for the second floor, that is the floor for
the four rooms each not less than fifty feet square in the
clear, and for the landing in the north, and the landing in
the south, of the building, where the stairs are to go up—
at this stage of the work, a chain, composed of bars of inch
square iron, each bar about ten feet long, and linked together by hooks formed of the ends of the bars, shall be
laid straightly and horizontally along the several walls, and
shall be as tightly as possible worked into the centre of
them throughout, and shall be secured wherever necessary,
especially at all the angles, by iron clamps solidly fastened,
so as to prevent cracking or swerving in any part; centres
shall then be laid, the proper arches turned for the second
floor and landings, and the second floor and landings shall
be laid: the outside and the inside walls shall then be
carried up of the same thickness of two feet throughout
as high as may be necessary to begin the recess intended
to fix the centres for the third floor and landings; and,
when so far carried up, another chain similar in all respects
to that used at the second story, shall be in like manner
worked into the walls throughout as tightly as possible,
and clamped in the same way with equal care; centres shall

9

be formed, the proper arches turned, and the third floor
and landings shall be laid: the outside and the inside walls
shall then be carried up, of the same thickness of two feet
throughout, as high as may be necessary to begin the recess intended to fix the centres for the roof; and, when so
carried up, a third chain, in all respects like those used
at the second and third stories, shall in the manner before
described be worked as tightly as possible into the walls
throughout, and shall be clamped with equal care; centres
shall now be fixed in the manner best adapted for the roof,
which is to form the ceiling for the third story, the proper
arches shall be turned, and the roof shall be laid as nearly
horizontally as may be, consistently with the easy passage
of water to the eaves: the outside walls, still of the thickness of two feet throughout, shall then be carried up about
two feet above the level of the platform, and shall have
marble capping, with a strong and neat iron railing thereon: The outside walls shall be faced with slabs or blocks
of marble or granite, not less than two feet thick, and
fastened together with clamps securely sunk therein—
they shall be carried up flush from the recess of one foot
formed at the first floor where the foundation outside wall
is reduced to two feet: The floors and landings as well as
the roof shall be covered with marble slabs, securely laid
in mortar; the slabs on the roof to be twice as thick as
those on the floors. In constructing the walls, as well as
in turning the arches, and laying the floors, landings, and
roof, good and strong mortar, and grout, shall be used,
so that no cavity whatever may any where remain. A
furnace or furnaces for the generation of heated air shall
be placed in the cellar, and the heated air shall be introduced in adequate quantity wherever wanted by means of

pipes and flues inserted and made for the purpose in the walls, and as those walls shall be constructed. In case it shall be found expedient, for the purposes of a library or otherwise, to encrease the number of rooms by dividing any of those, directed to be not less than fifty feet square in the clear, into parts, the partition walls to be of solid materials. A room most suitable for the purpose, shall be set apart for the reception and preservation of my books and papers, and I direct that they shall be placed there by my executors and carefully preserved therein. There shall be two principal doors of entrance into the college, one into the entry or hall on the first floor in the north of the building, and in the centre between the east and west walls, the other into the entry or hall in the south of the building, and in the centre between the east and west walls; the dimensions to be determined by a due regard to the size of the entire building, to that of the entry, and to the purposes of the doors. The necessity for, as well as the position and size of other doors, internal or external, and also the position and size of the windows, to be, in like manner, decided on by a consideration of the uses to which the building is to be applied, the size of the building itself and of the several rooms, and of the advantages of light and air: there should in each instance be double doors; those opening into the rooms to be what are termed glass doors, so as to encrease the quantity of light for each room, and those opening outward to be of substantial wood work well lined and secured: the windows of the second and third stories I recommend to be made in the style of those in the first and second stories of my present dwelling house North Water street, on the eastern front thereof; and outside each window I recommend that a substantial and neat

iron balcony be placed sufficiently wide to admit the opening of the shutters against the walls; the windows of the
lower story to be in the same style, except that they are not
to descend to the floor, but so far as the surbase, up to
which the wall is to be carried, as is the case in lower story
of my house at my place in Passyunk township. In mi-
nute particulars, not here noticed, utility and good taste
should determine. There should be at least four out-
buildings, detached from the main edifice and from each
other, and in such positions as shall at once answer the
purposes of the institution, and be consistent with the
symmetry of the whole establishment:—each building
should be, as far as practicable, devoted to a distinct purpose: in that one or more of those buildings, in which
they may be most useful, I direct my executors to place
my plate and furniture of every sort. The entire square,
formed by High and Chestnut streets, and Eleventh and
Twelfth streets, shall be enclosed with a solid wall, at least
fourteen inches thick and ten feet high, capped with
marble and guarded with irons on the top so as to prevent
persons from getting over: there shall be two places of
entrance into the square, one in the centre of the wall
facing High street, and the other in the centre of the wall
facing Chestnut street: at each place of entrance there
shall be two gates, one opening inward and the other outward; those opening inward to be of iron and in the style
of the gates north and south of my banking house, and
those opening outward to be of substantial wood work
well lined and secured on the faces thereof with sheet iron.
The messuages now erected on the south-east corner of
High and Twelfth streets, and on Twelfth street, to be
taken down and removed, as soon as the College and out-

buildings shall have been erected, so that the establishment may be rendered secure and private.

When the college and appurtenances shall have been constructed, and supplied with plain and suitable furniture, and books, philosophical and experimental instruments and apparatus, and all other matters needful to carry my general design into execution; the income issues and profits of so much of the said sum of two millions of dollars as shall remain unexpended shall be applied to maintain the said College according to my directions:

1. The institution shall be organized as soon as practicable and, to accomplish that purpose more effectually, due public notice of the intended opening of the college shall be given—so that there may be an opportunity to make selections of competent instructors, and other agents, and those who may have the charge of orphans may be aware of the provisions intended for them:

2. A competent number of instructors, teachers, assistants and other necessary agents, shall be selected, and when needful their places from time to time supplied: they shall receive adequate compensation for their services: but no person shall be employed who shall not be of tried skill in his or her proper department, of established moral character—and in all cases persons shall be chosen on account of their merit, and not through favor or intrigue.

3. As many poor white male orphans,[1] between the ages of six and ten years, as the said income shall be adequate to maintain, shall be introduced into the college as soon as possible; and from time to time as there may be va-

---

[1] A fatherless child, Soohan *vs.* City, 33 Penna. State Reports, p. 9.

cancies, or as increased ability from income may warrant, others shall be introduced.

4. On the application for admission, an accurate statement should be taken, in a book prepared for the purpose, of the name, birth-place, age, health, condition as to relatives, and other particulars, useful to be known, of each orphan.

5. No orphan should be admitted until the guardians or directors of the poor, or a proper guardian, or other competent authority,[1] shall have given, by indenture, relinquishment, or otherwise, adequate power to the Mayor Aldermen and citizens of Philadelphia, or to directors or others by them appointed, to enforce, in relation to each orphan, every proper restraint, and to prevent relatives or others from interfering with or withdrawing such orphan from the institution.

6. Those orphans, for whose admission application shall first be made, shall be first introduced, all other things concurring—and at all future times priority of application shall entitle the applicant to preference in admission, all other things concurring: but, if there shall be at any time, more applicants than vacancies, and the applying orphans shall have been born in different places, a preference shall be given,—*first* to orphans born in the city of Philadelphia;[2] *secondly*, to those born in any other part of Pennsylvania; *thirdly* to those born in the city of New York (that being the first port on the continent of North America, at which I arrived); and *lastly*, to those born in

---

[1] The mother, guardian, or next friend may bind to the City, Act of Assembly approved May 23, 1887 (P.L., 1887, p. 168).

[2] The "old City" with limits as they existed at the death of Mr. Girard, Soohan *vs.* City, 33 Penna. State-Reports, p. 9.

the city of New Orleans, being the first port on the said continent at which I first traded, in the first instance as first officer, and subsequently as master and part owner of a vessel and cargo.

7. The orphans, admitted into the College, shall be there fed with plain but wholesome food, clothed with plain but decent apparel (no distinctive dress ever to be worn) and lodged in a plain but safe manner: Due regard shall be paid to their health, and to this end their persons and clothes shall be kept clean, and they shall have suitable and rational exercise and recreation: They shall be instructed in the various branches of a sound education, comprehending reading, writing, grammar, arithmetic, geography, navigation, surveying, practical mathematics, astronomy, natural, chemical, and experimental philosophy, the French and Spanish languages [I do not forbid, but I do not recommend, the Greek and Latin Languages]—and such other learning and science, as the capacities of the several scholars may merit or warrant: I would have them taught facts and things, rather than words or signs: And, especially, I desire, that by every proper means a pure attachment to our republican institutions, and to the sacred rights of conscience, as guaranteed by our happy constitutions, shall be formed and fostered in the minds of the scholars.

8. Should it unfortunately happen, that any of the orphans, admitted into the college, shall, from malconduct, have become unfit companions for the rest, and mild means of reformation prove abortive, they should no longer remain therein.

9. Those scholars, who shall merit it, shall remain in the college until they shall respectively arrive at between four-

teen and eighteen years of age; they shall then be bound
out by the Mayor, Aldermen and citizens of Philadelphia,
or under their direction, to suitable occupations, as those
of agriculture, navigation, arts, mechanical trades, and
manufactures, according to the capacities and acquire-
ments of the scholars respectively; consulting, as far as
prudence shall justify it, the inclinations of the several
scholars, as to the occupation, art, or trade, to be learned.

In relation to the organization of the college and its
appendages, I leave, necessarily, many details to the Mayor
Aldermen and citizens of Philadelphia and their successors;
and I do so, with the more confidence, as, from the nature
of my bequests and the benefit to result from them, I trust
that my fellow citizens of Philadelphia, will observe and
evince especial care and anxiety in selecting members for
their City Councils, and other agents: There are, however,
some restrictions, which I consider it my duty to prescribe,
and to be, amongst others, conditions on which my bequest for said college is made and to be enjoyed, namely:
first, I enjoin and require, that, if, at the close of any year,
the income of the fund devoted to the purposes of the said
college shall be more than sufficient for the maintenance
of the institution during that year, then the balance of the
said income, after defraying such maintenance, shall be
forthwith invested in good securities, thereafter to be and
remain a part of the capital; but, in no event, shall any
part of the said capital be sold, disposed of, or pledged, to
meet the current expenses of the said institution, to which
I devote the interest, income, and dividends thereof exclusively: *secondly*, I enjoin and require, that *no ecclesiastic,
missionary, or minister of any sect whatsoever, shall ever hold
or exercise any station or duty whatever in the said college;*

nor shall any such person ever be admitted for any purpose, **or** *as a visitor, within the premises appropriated to the purposes of the said college:—. . . .* In making this restriction, I do not mean to cast any reflection upon any sect or person whatsoever; **but, as there is such** a multitude of sects, and **such a diversity of opinion amongst them, I desire to keep the tender minds of the** orphans, **who are to derive** advantage from this bequest, free from the ex**citements,** which clashing doctrines and sectarian controversy are so apt to produce; My desire is, that all the instructors and teachers in the college shall take pains to **instil** into the minds of the scholars *the purest principles of morality,* so that, on their entrance into active life, they may, *from inclination and habit,* evince *benevolence towards their fellow creatures,* and *a* **love of truth**, *sobriety* **and** *industry*, adopting at the same time such religious tenets **as** their *matured reason* may **enable them to prefer.**

. . . . . . If the income, arising from **that part of** the said sum of two millions of dollars, remaining after the construction and furnishing of the college and out-buildings, shall, owing to the encrease of the number of orphans, applying for admission, or other cause, be inadequate to the construction of new buildings, or the maintenance and education of **as many** orphans as may apply **for admission, then** such further sum as may be necessary **for the construction of new** buildings and the maintenance **and education** of such further number of orphans, as can **be maintained** and instructed within such buildings as **the said** square of ground shall be adequate to, shall be taken from **the** final residuary fund hereinafter expressly referred to for **the purpose,** comprehending the **income of** my real estate **in the city and county** of Philadelphia, **and** the divi-

dends of my stock in the Schuylkill navigation company
—my design and desire being, that the benefits of said institution shall be extended to as great a number of orphans
as the limits of the said square and buildings therein can
accommodate.

XXII.   And as to the further sum of *five hundred thousand dollars*, part of the residue of my personal estate, in
trust, to invest the same securely, and to keep the same
so invested, and to apply the income thereof exclusively
to the following purposes, that is to say:

1. To lay out, regulate, curb, light and pave a passage
or street, on the east part of the city of Philadelphia, fronting the river Delaware, not less than twenty-one feet
wide, and to be called *Delaware Avenue*, extending from
South or Cedar Street, all along the east part of Water
street squares, and the west side of the logs, which form
the heads of the docks, or thereabouts; and to this intent
to obtain such acts of Assembly, and to make such pur-
chases or agreements, as will enable the Mayor Aldermen
and citizens of Philadelphia to remove or pull down all
the buildings, fences and obstructions, which may be in
the way, and to prohibit all buildings, fences, or erections
of any kind to the eastward of said avenue;—to fill up the
heads of such of the docks as may not afford sufficient
room for the said street;—to compel the owners of
wharves to keep them clean and covered completely with
gravel or other hard materials, and to be so levelled that
water will not remain thereon after a shower of rain,—to
completely clean [1] and keep clean all the docks within the

---

[1] Not to clean, but to compel the owners to clean, Beck *vs.* City, 17 Penna.
State Reports, p. 104.

limits of the city, fronting on the Delaware;—and to pull down all platforms carried out, from the east part of the city over the river Delaware, on piles or pillars.

2. To pull down and remove all wooden buildings (as well those made of wood and other combustible materials, as those called brick-paned or frame buildings filled in with bricks) that are erected within the limits of the City of Philadelphia—and also to prohibit the erection of any such buildings within the said city's limits at any future time.

3. To regulate, widen, pave, and curb Water street, and to distribute the Schuylkill water therein upon the following plan that is to say, ... that Water street be widened east and west from Vine street all the way to South street, in like manner as it is from the front of my dwelling to the front of my stores on the west side of Water street, and the regulation of the curbstones continued at the same distance from one another, as they are at present opposite to the said dwelling and stores, so that the regulation of the said street be not less than thirty-nine feet wide, and afford a large and convenient foot-way, clear of obstructions and incumbrances of every nature, and the cellar doors on which, if any shall be permitted, not to extend from the buildings on to the foot-way more than four feet; the said width to be encreased gradually, as the fund shall permit, and as the capacity to remove impediments shall encrease, until there shall be a correct and permanent regulation of Water street on the principles above stated. so that it may run north and south as strait as possible: That the ten feet middle alleys, belonging to the public, and running from the centre of the east squares to Front street, all the way down across Water street to the river Delaware, be kept open and cleansed as city property, all

the way from Vine to South street—that such part of each
centre or middle alley as runs from Front to Water street
be arched over with bricks or stone, in so strong a manner
as to facilitate the building of plain and permanent stone
steps and plat-forms, so that they may be washed and kept
constantly clean: and that the continuance of the said
alleys, from the east side of Water street be curbed all the
way to the river Delaware and kept open forever—. . . .
(I understand that those middle or centre alleys were left
open in the first plan of the lots, on the east front of the
city, which were granted from the east side of Front street
to the river Delaware, and that each lot on said east front
has contributed to make those alleys by giving a part of
their ground in proportion to the size of each lot; those
alleys were in the first instance, and still are, considered
public property, intended for the convenience of the inhabitants residing in Front street to go down to the river
for water and other purposes; but, owing to neglect or to
some other cause, on the part of those, who have had the
care of the city property, several encroachments have been
made on them by individuals, by wholly occupying, or
building over, them, or otherwise, and in that way the
inhabitants, more particularly those who reside in the
neighborhood, are deprived of the benefit of that wholesome air, which their opening and cleansing throughout
would afford): That the iron pipes, in Water street, which,
by being of smaller size than those in the other streets,
and too near the surface of the ground, cause constant
leaks, particularly in the winter season, which in many
places render the street impassable, be taken up and re-
placed by pipes of the same size quality and dimensions
in every respect, and laid down as deeply from the surface

of the ground, as the iron pipes, which are laid in the main
streets of the City: . . . . and as it respects pumps for
Schuylkill water and fire-plugs in Water street, that one
of each be fixed at the south-west corner of Vine and
Water streets, and so running southward, one of each near
the steps of the centre alley going up to Front street; one
of each at the south-west corner of Sassafras and Water
streets, one of each near the steps of the centre alley going
up to Front street, and so on at every south-west corner of
all the main streets and Water street, and of the centre
alleys of every square, as far as South or Cedar street; and
when the same shall have been completed, that all Water
street shall be repaved by the best workmen in the most
complete manner, with the best paving water-stones, after
the height of the curbstones shall have been regulated
throughout, as well as the ascent and descent of the street,
in such manner as to conduct the Water through the main
streets and the centre alleys to the river Delaware, as far
as practicable; and whenever any part of the street shall
want to be raised, to use nothing but good paving gravel
for that purpose, so as to make the paving as permanent
as possible: . . . . By all which improvements, it is my intention to place and maintain the section of the city above
referred to in a condition which will correspond better with
the general cleanness and appearance of the whole city,
and be more consistent with the safety, health, and comfort of the citizens.   And my mind and will are, that all
the income, interest and dividends of the said capital sum
of five hundred thousand dollars shall be yearly and every
year expended upon the said objects, in the order in which
I have stated them as closely as possible, and upon no
other objects until those enumerated shall have been at-

tained: and, when those objects shall have been accomplished, I authorise and direct the said The Mayor Aldermen and Citizens to apply such part of the income of the said capital sum of five hundred thousand dollars as they may think proper to the further improvement, from time to time, of the eastern or Delaware front of the City.

XXIII.   I give and bequeath to the Commonwealth of Pennsylvania, the sum of *three hundred thousand dollars*, for the purposes of internal improvement by canal navigation, to be paid into the state treasury by my executors, as soon as such laws shall have been enacted by the constituted authorities of the said commonwealth as shall be necessary, and amply sufficient to carry into effect, or to enable the constituted authorities of the city of Philadelphia to carry into effect, the several improvements above specified; namely, 1. *laws*, to cause Delaware avenue, as above described, to be made, paved, curbed, and lighted; to cause the buildings, fences, and other obstructions now existing to be abated and removed; and to prohibit the erection of any such obstructions to the eastward of said Delaware avenue; 2. *laws*, to cause all wooden buildings as above described to be removed, and to prohibit their future erection within the limits of the city of Philadelphia: 3. *laws*, providing for the gradual widening, regulating, paving, and curbing Water street, as hereinbefore described, and also for the repairing the middle alleys, and introducing the Schuylkill water, and pumps, as before specified—all which objects, may, I persuade myself, be accomplished on principles at once just into relation to individuals, and highly beneficial to the public: the said sum, however, not to be paid, unless said laws be passed within one year after my decease.

XXIV.   And as it regards *the remainder of said residue* of my personal estate, in trust, to invest the same in good securities, and in like manner to invest the interest and income thereof from time to time, so that the whole shall form a permanent fund; and to apply the income of the said fund:—

1. To the further improvement and maintenance of the aforesaid College, as directed in the last paragraph of the XXIst clause of this will:

2. To enable the Corporation of the city of Philadelphia to provide more effectually than they now do, for the security of the persons and property of the inhabitants of the said city, by a competent police, including a sufficient number of watchmen really suited to the purpose; and to this end, I recommend a division of the city, into watch districts or four parts, each under a proper head, and that at least two watchmen shall in each round or station patrol together.

3. To enable the said corporation to improve the city property, and the general appearance of the city itself; and, in effect to diminish the burden of taxation, now most oppressive especially on those, who are the least able to bear it:

To all which objects, the prosperity of the City, and the health and comfort of its inhabitants, I devote the said fund as aforesaid, and direct the income thereof to be applied yearly and every year for ever—after providing for the College as hereinbefore directed, as my primary object.   But, if the said city shall knowingly and wilfully violate any of the conditions hereinbefore and hereinafter mentioned, then I give and bequeath the said remainder and accumulations to the Commonwealth of Pennsylvania,

for the purposes of internal navigation, excepting however the rents issues and profits of my real estate in the
City and County of Philadelphia, which shall forever be
reserved and applied to maintain the aforesaid College, in
the manner specified in the last paragraph of the XXIst
clause of this will: And, if the Commonwealth of Pennsylvania shall fail to apply this or the preceding bequest
to the purposes before mentioned, or shall apply any part
thereof to any other use, or shall for the term of one year,
from the time of my decease, fail or omit to pass the laws
hereinbefore specified for promoting the improvement of
the city of Philadelphia, then I give devise and bequeath
the said remainder and accumulations (the rents aforesaid
always excepted and reserved for the College as aforesaid)
to the United States of America for the purposes of internal navigation and no other.

Provided, nevertheless, and I do hereby declare, that all
the preceding bequests and devises of the residue of my
estate to The Mayor Aldermen and Citizens of Philadelphia, are made upon the following express conditions, that
is to say—*First,* That none of the monies, principal, interest, dividends, or rents, arising from the said residuary
devise and bequest, shall at any time be applied to any
other purpose or purposes whatever than those herein
mentioned and appointed:—*Second,* that separate accounts, distinct from the other accounts of the corporation, shall be kept by the said corporation, concerning the
said devise, bequest, college and funds, and of the investment and application thereof; and that a separate account
or accounts of the same shall be kept in bank, not blended
with any other account, so that it may at all times appear
on examination by a committee of the legislature as here-

inafter mentioned, that my intentions had been **fully complied** with:—*Third*, That the said corporation render a detailed account annually in duplicate to the legislature of the Commonwealth of Pennsylvania, at the commencement **of the session, one copy for the senate and the other for the house of representatives, concerning the said devised and bequeathed estate, and the investment and application of the same, and** also a report in like manner of the state of the said College, and **shall** submit all their **books** papers and accounts touching **the** same, to a committee **or** committees of the legislature for examination, **when the** same shall be required: *Fourth*, The said corporation shall also cause to be published in the month of January, annually, in two **or** more newspapers **printed in** the city of Philadelphia, a concise but plain account **of the state of the trusts, devises, and bequests herein declared and made, comprehending the condition of the said** college, the number of **scholars, and other** particulars needful to be publicly known, for the **year next** preceding the said month of January, **annually.**

XXV. And whereas **I have executed** an assignment in **trust of my banking** establishment, to take effect the day before **my decease, to the intent that all the** concerns **thereof may be closed by themselves, without being blended with the concerns of my general estate, and the balance remaining to be paid over to my executors: Now, I do** hereby direct **my executors, hereinafter mentioned, not to** interfere with the said trust in any way except to see **that** the same is faithfully executed, **and to aid the execution thereof by** all such acts and deeds **as may be necessary and expedient** to effectuate the same, **so that it may be speedily closed, and the balance** paid over to my executors, **to go,** as in my will, into the residue of my estate: And I do hereby authorise direct and empower the said trustees from time to time, as the capital of the said bank shall be received, and shall not be wanted for the discharge of the debts due thereat, to invest the same in good securities in the names of my executors, and to hand over the same to them, to be disposed of according to this my will.

XXVI. Lastly—I do hereby nominate and appoint Timothy Paxson, Thomas P. Cope, Joseph Roberts, William J. Duane, and John A. Barclay . . . . executors of this my last will and testament: I recommend to them to close the concerns of my estate as expeditiously as possible, and to see that my intentions in respect to the residue of my estate are and shall be strictly complied with: and I do hereby revoke all other wills by me heretofore made.

In witness, I, the said Stephen Girard have to this my last will and testament, contained in thirty-five pages, set my hand at the bottom of each page, and my hand and seal at the bottom of this page; the said will executed, from motives of prudence, in duplicate, this sixteenth day of February, in the year one thousand eight hundred and thirty.

STEPHEN GIRARD. [SEAL]

Signed, sealed, published, and declared by the said Stephen Girard, as and for his last will and testament, in the presence of us, who have at his request hereunto subscribed our names as witnesses thereto in the presence of the said testator and of each other, February 16, 1830.

JOHN H. IRWIN,
SAML ARTHUR,
S. H. CARPENTER.

Whereas I, Stephen Girard, the testator named in the foregoing will and testament, dated the sixteenth day of February eighteen hundred and thirty, have, since the execution thereof, purchased several parcels and pieces of real estate, and have built sundry messuages, all which, as well as any real estate that I may hereafter purchase, it is my wish and intention to pass by the said will, now I do hereby republish the foregoing last will and testament dated February 16, 1830, and do confirm the same in all particulars: In witness, I the said Stephen Girard set my hand and seal hereunto the twenty-fifth day of December eighteen hundred and thirty.

STEPHEN GIRARD. [SEAL]

Signed sealed published and declared by the said Stephen Girard as and for a re-publication of his last will and testament in the presence of us, who at his request have hereunto subscribed our names as witnesses thereto in the presence of the said testator and of each other, Decr 25, 1830.

JOHN H. IRWIN,
SAML ARTHUR,
JNO. THOMSON.

Whereas I, Stephen Girard, the testator named in the foregoing will and testament, dated February 16, 1830, have, since the execution thereof, purchased several parcels and pieces of land and real estate, and have built sundry messuages, all which, as well as any real estate that I may hereafter purchase, it is my intention to pass by said will; and whereas, in particular, I have recently purchased from Mr William Parker the mansion house, out-buildings, and forty-five acres and some perches of land, called Peel Hall, on the Ridge Road in Penn Township, now I declare it to be my intention and I direct that the orphan establishment, provided for in my said will, instead of being built as therein directed upon my square of ground between High and Chestnut and Eleventh and Twelfth streets in the city of Philadelphia, shall be built upon the estate so purchased from M[r] W. Parker, and I hereby devote the said estate to that purpose[1] exclusively in the same manner as I had devoted the said square, hereby directing that all the improvements and arrangements for the said Orphan Establishment prescribed by my said will as to said square shall be made and executed upon the said estate, just as if I had in my will devoted the said estate to said purpose—consequently the said square of ground is to constitute and I declare it to be a part of the residue and remainder of my real and personal estate and given and devised for the same uses and purposes as are declared in section XX. of my will, it being my intention that the said square of ground shall be built upon and improved in such a manner as to secure a safe and permanent income for the purposes stated in said XXth section: In witness whereof I, the said Stephen Girard set my hand and seal hereunto the twentieth day of June eighteen hundred and thirty-one.

STEPHEN GIRARD. [SEAL]

Signed sealed published and declared by the said Stephen Girard as and for a re-publication of his last will and testament and a further direction in relation to the real

---

[1] Streets not to be laid out or passed through, unless so recommended by Trustees or Directors of College, Act, March 24, 1832 (P. L., 1831–32, p. 176).

estate therein mentioned, in the presence of us who at his request have hereunto subscribed our names as witnesses thereto in the presence of the said testator and of each other, June 20, 1831.

S. H. CARPENTER,
L. BARDIN,
SAML ARTHUR.

Acts of Assembly to enable the City to carry the Will into effect were approved—

March 24, 1832 (P.L., 1831–32, p. 176);
April 4, 1832 (P.L., 1831–32, p. 275);
February 27, 1847 (P.L., 1847, p. 178).

GIRARD COLLEGE: ITS ORGANIZATION AND ADMINISTRATION

BY WILLIAM H. ZELLER, '72.

Four distinct periods divide the record of the administration and the government of Girard College between the years 1832 and 1898. The first continued from 1832 to 1847, under the direction of a Board of Directors of Girard Trusts; the second from 1847 to 1856, under the administration of a Board of Directors; the third from 1856 to 1870, under the supervision of a Board of Directors elected by the Councils of the consolidated city of Philadelphia, and the fourth, from 1870 to date, under the supervision of the Board of Directors of City Trusts as now constituted.

Doubt and uncertainty seem to have been in the public mind concerning the intentions of Mr. Girard as expressed in his last will and testament.

Probably none beyond the executors, and the eminent attorney who assisted in the preparation of the will, were acquainted with the plan Mr. Girard had in view for the establishment of his great charity. The knowledge of his intentions in disposing of his vast fortune was apparently but vaguely understood or appreciated even by these, and the first practical steps for executing the terms of the bequest were not taken by the Councils of the city of Philadelphia until January 31, 1833.

154

The will had been signed on February 16, 1830, and the codicil changing the location of the College from the block bounded by High (Market), Chestnut, Eleventh and Twelfth Streets to Peel Hall, on the Ridge Road in Penn Township, was added June 20, 1831. Letters testamentary were granted December 31, 1831.

On January 9, 1832, the Councils of the city passed a resolution appointing a committee of five to report what measures should be taken to execute the trusts created by Mr. Girard. The Committee made a number of reports, and on October 1, 1832, submitted an ordinance creating the Commissioners of the Girard Trusts. This ordinance was amended on December 13, 1832, and a Board of Trustees, with Nicholas Biddle as Chairman, was elected on February 11, 1833. Under a resolution adopted by Councils on June 8, 1832, a committee of six was appointed to advertise for plans for the College buildings. No haste seems to have marked the labors of this Committee, for it was not until the joint meeting of the Building Committee and the Board of Directors in April, 1833, that final action was taken upon this subject.

Throughout the year 1832 nothing was accomplished to determine some definite plan to make the provisions of the will practicable and operative. This seeming inactivity of the executors was a subject of irritation in the public mind, but the intricate situation was finally solved, and public interest gratified, by a statement made in December, 1832, that the executors were ready to suggest a preliminary stage for legislation by Councils.

While matters had proceeded heretofore in no spirit of haste, as the executors of the will doubtless believed in cautious measures for the interpretation of each provision, a contrary course now appears to have governed the authorities. The Joint Committee met for the first time on April 5, 1833, followed, after organization, by a second meeting on April 18, at which time the architect was instructed to submit plans for the Main Building. That these plans were prepared with great speed is demonstrated by the fact that they were adopted on April 29, eleven days after the organization of the two bodies constituting the controlling power. This exceptional process in determining a proceeding so momentous, as the preparation and submission of plans for the construction of the Main Building, was mentioned by Mr. Thomas U. Walter, the architect, in his yearly reports as an error, and as the cause of much contention and complication in the progress of the work. It was, however, in accordance with the feverish condition of the public mind. Everybody demanded the rapid fulfilment of the design of Mr. Girard.

With the submission of the architect's plans on April 29 came the excavations for the foundations begun on May 6, and on July 4, 1833, the laying of the corner-stone. November 13, 1847, marked the period of the conclusion of the labors of the Building Committee, just fourteen years and six months after it had been called into existence, and the final report of this Committee was made, on that date, through John C. Davis, Chairman, in accordance with the ordinance of Councils passed on September 16, directing the Committee to give possession of the College to the Directors.

The Trustees had been anxious that some part of the Estate should be devoted to the purposes of the Founder as soon as possible. In 1836 Alexander Dallas Bache had been elected President, and in 1838 they endeavored to open a part of the College to meet the purposes of the will; but eminent legal authority, in John Sergeant and Horace Binney, gave an opinion that no part of the grounds could be opened until the buildings were entirely completed.

The organization of the College was begun by the adoption of an ordinance of Councils on May 27, 1847, authorizing the election of a Board of Directors of sixteen persons, who governed the College from November, 1847, until June, 1856, when by another ordinance of Councils the system was changed to conform with the Act of Consolidation of the city passed in 1854. An ordinance passed November 9, 1848, constituted Councils a standing Committee of Visitation.

During the nine years of the existence of the first Board of Directors there were thirty-nine members,—changes being frequent, not a few serving but a year and some only a few months. The only surviving member of this Board is Mr. Frederick Fraley. The ordinance of June, 1856, changed the system of government of the College to conform to the Act of Consolidation, and the Board of Directors was increased to eighteen members. Under it the first Board was chosen in June, 1856, and organized with William Biddle as President. So far as known, the only survivors of this Board—a total of sixty-nine members from 1856 to 1869, when the Board of Directors of City Trusts assumed control under Act of Assembly approved June 30, 1869—are:

HENRY C. CORFIELD
WILLIAM C. HAINES
ROBERT T. GILL

JOSEPH R. RHOADS
AUGUST HEATON
WILLIAM E. LITTLETON

Mr. Littleton enjoys the distinction of being the only member of the Girard College Alumni ever serving as a Director.

The Board of Directors of City Trusts was created by an Act of the Legislature amending the charter of the city of Philadelphia, approved June 30, 1869.

Frequent changes in the city Councils had given a more or less partisan character to the various appointments to the old Board of Directors, and the difficulty of securing appropriations commensurate with the needs of the Institution, together with what has been charged as indifference to the future of the several trusts, led to statements of neglect and charges of the existence of abuse in their administration. It was considered best to secure legislative action, and to remove the care of the College, and of the several trusts, from the superintendence of the city Councils by creating a new department; and these changes introduce the fourth period of government,—the present system, now entering upon its twenty-ninth year. That the wisdom of the advocates of this change has been abundantly proven and justified is evidenced by an increase in the value of the Girard Estate and of the other trusts more than fourfold.

The appointments to this Board were made by the Judges of the Supreme Court of the Commonwealth, together with the Judges of the District Court and of the Court of Common Pleas of the City and County of Philadelphia, and on September 2, 1869, J. Ross Snowden, Prothonotary of the Supreme Court, notified the members of the original Board of their appointment,—the Mayor of the city and the Presidents of Select and Common Councils being members for the terms of their office, and the twelve citizens during good behavior.

The Board organized September 13, 1869, by the election of William Welsh as President. Being informed that on July 8, 1869, the Councils of the city had instructed the officers superintending the various charities not to acknowledge the new authority, nor to transfer to it any of the property of the trusts, to test the constitutionality of the law creating this Board, a Committee, consisting of Edward King, James L. Claghorn, John H. Michener, and William Welsh, was appointed to take whatever measures might be necessary to make the law operative. The city having employed William M. Meredith, Franklin B. Gowan, Edward Omstead, and John Goforth as their counsel to contest the law, this Committee employed William Strong, Peter McCall, and John Fallen to represent the Board of Directors of City Trusts.

An early hearing before the Supreme Court was had, and on February 17, 1870, Justice Sharswood delivered the unanimous opinion of the Court confirming the validity of the law. The city failing to comply with the decision of the Court, F. Carroll Brewster, the permanent counsel of the Board, applied for a writ directing obedience to the decision. This writ having been granted, the city withdrew its opposition, and the Board assumed control, taking possession of all the property on February 25, 1870, and appointing the necessary committees to ascertain the condition of the various trusts and to determine the best plan for their administration.

One of the earliest difficulties experienced was the absence of a condensed statement of the various trusts (which in 1870 were twenty-nine in number, six having been added since that year), and a Committee was appointed to prepare a history of them.

From the beginning, those in control of the administration and government of the College have been representative men of the city who had won public confidence,
and attained public honors, by their integrity of character;
but it is a matter of more than passing note that the Board
of Directors of City Trusts has, by its purity of business
methods and its clearness of business judgment, wrought
out a stewardship without parallel in the history of any
similar body.

The uncertain tenure of the term of office common to
the Directorate in the periods from 1833 to 1869 inter-
fered materially with the success of the great plan so won-
derfully outlined by Mr. Girard in his will. The question
of partisan preferment naturally entered into the action
of Councils and in the selection for members of the trust,
and continually led to complications and indecisions in
the prosecution of the work on the buildings, and later in
the carrying forward of the course of instruction and of
the affairs of the household of the College. Under such
ephemeral conditions and with this environment of in-
stability of system and of methods, the situation demanded
a change, which the Legislature of Pennsylvania, in its
prerogative, made by the creation of the present board of
administration.

The membership of the several bodies comprising the
administrative and governing power of the Girard Estate
and of Girard College from the year 1832 to the year 1898
is given in the annexed statement:

COMMISSIONERS FOR THE MANAGEMENT OF THE GIRARD TRUSTS.

(Under Ordinance of Councils passed September 15, 1832. Appointed by Councils, October 1, 1832.)

JAMES PAGE
WILLIAM E. LEHMAN
THOMAS DUNLAP
JOHN M. HOOD
JOHN MOSS

JOSHUA LIPPINCOTT
ROBERTS VAUX
MICHAEL BAKER
JOSEPH WORRELL

BOARD OF DIRECTORS OF GIRARD TRUSTS.

(Under Amended Ordinance of Councils, December 13, 1832. Elected by Councils, February 11, 1833.)

NICHOLAS BIDDLE
WILLIAM H. KEATING
ALGERNON S. ROBERTS
CHARLES BIRD
DR. JOHN M. KEAGY
DR. GEORGE B. WOOD
RICHARD PRICE
JOHN C. STOCKER

JOSEPH McILVAIN
WILLIAM M. MEREDITH
DR. THOMAS McEUEN
BENJAMIN W. RICHARDS
THOMAS DUNLAP
GEORGE W. TOLAND
JOHN STEELE

BOARD OF TRUSTEES.

(Under Ordinance, January 31, 1833. Elected *by Councils, March 28, 1833.)*

NICHOLAS BIDDLE
BENJAMIN W. RICHARDS
JOHN STEELE
JOSEPH McILVAINE

DR. THOMAS McEUEN
THOMAS DUNLAP
WILLIAM M. MEREDITH
RICHARD PRICE

LATER APPOINTMENTS WERE:

GEORGE B. WOOD
ALGERNON S. ROBERTS
SAMUEL V. MERRICK
WILLIAM W. HALY
MATTHIAS W. BALDWIN
CHARLES D. MEIGS
HENRY TROTH
JOHN SWIFT
JOSEPH R. INGERSOLL

HENRY TROTH
CHARLES BIRD
GEORGE W. TOLAND
JOHN K. KANE
JOHN B. ELLISON
JOSIAH RANDALL
WILLIAM S. PEROT
WILLIAM D. BRINCKLE

THE BUILDING COMMITTEE.

(Under Ordinance of Councils, January 31, 1833.)

JOHN GILDER, *Chairman*

JOSHUA LIPPINCOTT

DENNIS McCREDY

JOHN BYERLY

JOHN R. NEFF

JOSEPH WORRELL

SAMUEL V. MERRICK

EPHRAIM HAINS

JAMES BURK

PETER WRIGHT

JOHN M. BARCLAY

ISAAC ROACH

HENRY SAILOR

ISAAC OTIS

WILLIAM V. ANDERSON

JOHN WEIGAND

ISAAC ELLIOTT

JOHN S. WARNER

CORNELIUS TIERS

JOHN LINDSAY

DAVID WINEBRENER

JAMES HUTCHINSON

GEORGE SHARSWOOD

JAMES ANDREWS

SAMUEL W. WEER

WILLIAM MORRIS

JAMES Y. HUMPHREYS

JOHN C. DAVIS

JAMES ROWLAND

MATTHEW NEWKIRK

JOHN PRICE WETHERILL

JAMES J. BOSWELL

JACOB E. HAGERT

GIDEON SCULL

PETER McCALL

JAMES LESLIE

ISAAC BARTON

JOHN AGNEW

ALGERNON S. ROBERTS

JOHN RODMAN PAUL

JACOB AMOS

ROBERT HUTCHINSON

WILLIAM W. HALY

JOSEPH B. SMITH

BOARD OF DIRECTORS OF GIRARD COLLEGE, 1847–1856.

(Elected under Ordinance of City Councils, May 27, 1847, providing for sixteen members.)

WILLIAM BIDDLE

JAMES J. BOSWELL

THOMAS P. COPE

MORDECAI L. DAWSON

WILLIAM J. DUANE

FREDERICK FRALEY

CHARLES GILPIN

ALEXANDER HENRY

SAUNDERS LEWIS

E. JOY MORRIS

SAMUEL NORRIS

JOHN RODMAN PAUL

SAMUEL H. PERKINS

GEORGE W. TOLAND

THOMAS U. WALTER

JOHN WEIGAND

JOSEPH R. CHANDLER

JAMES ROWLAND

JOSEPH COWPERTHWAIT

JOSEPH G. CLARKSON

WILLIAM WELSH

JAMES HUTCHINSON

JAMES R. GEMMILL

THOMAS G. HOLLINGSWORTH

WILLIAM MARTIN

ARTHUR G. COFFIN

FREDERICK A. PACKARD
ALGERNON S. ROBERTS
EDWARD Y. FARQUHAR
THOMAS ROBINS
DR. ALFRED E. ELWYN
THOMAS J. PERKINS
CHARLES A. POULSON

JOHN YARROW
JOHN W. RYAN
WILLIAM S. SMITH.
FRANCIS B. WARNER
JOHN U. GILLER
WILLIAM MARTIN

BOARD OF DIRECTORS OF THE GIRARD COLLEGE, 1856–1869.

(Elected under Ordinance of City Councils, June 19, 1856, providing for eighteen members.)

WILLIAM BIDDLE
MORDECAI L. DAWSON
WILLIAM J. DUANE
HENRY D. GILPIN
DANIEL DEAL
WILLIAM H. HAMILTON
JAMES MARTIN
WILLIAM MARTIN
DR. WILLIAM MAYBURRY
DR. GEORGE W. NEBINGER
FREDERICK A. PACKARD
HENRY M. PHILLIPS
THOMAS ROBINS
JOHN ROBBINS, JR.
THOMAS S. STEWART
JAMES S. WATSON
WILLIAM WELSH
SAMUEL H. PERKINS
JAMES J. BOSWELL
GEORGE C. BOWER, JR.
ALEXANDER BROWN
JAMES CAMPBELL
WILLIAM H. DRAYTON
SAMUEL FLOOD
DANIEL M. FOX
THOMAS E. HARKINS
ROBERT SELFRIDGE
RICHARD VAUX
CHARLES R. TREGO
AUGUSTUS HEATON

DR. CHARLES M. JACKSON
ALBERT C. ROBERTS
E. HARPER JEFFRIES
MORTON MCMICHAEL
HENRY C. CORFIELD
ROBERT M. FOUST
DR. HENRY YALE SMITH
JAMES PETERS
JOHN H. BRINGHURST
WILLIAM DIVINE
JOHN O. JAMES
WILLIAM BRADFORD
DR. WILLIAM W. BURNELL
JOHN FEST
FRANCIS P. MAGEE
LUTHER MARTIN
GUSTAVUS REMAK
WILLIAM H. KEICHLINE
DR. JOSEPH SITES
JOHN M. BUTLER
CHARLES E. LEX
ROBERT T. GILL
CHRISTIAN J. HOFFMAN
HORATIO GATES JONES
JOSEPH MOORE
THOMAS M. COLEMAN
JOHN FRY
WILLIAM C. HAINES
CYRUS HORNE
GEORGE REMSEN

JOSEPH R. RHOADS
HENRY SIMONS
EDWARD BAINS
THORNTON CONROW
GEORGE TRUMAN, JR.

THOMAS B. REEVES
ENOCH TAYLOR
ROBERT P. GILLINGHAM
WILLIAM E. LITTLETON
ALGERNON S. ROBERTS

PRESIDENTS OF THE BOARD OF DIRECTORS OF GIRARD COLLEGE.

JOSEPH R. CHANDLER
FREDERICK FRALEY
SAMUEL NORRIS
SAMUEL H. PERKINS
MORTON MCMICHAEL

RICHARD VAUX
CHARLES E. LEX
ROBERT M. FOUST
AUGUSTUS HEATON

THE BOARD OF DIRECTORS OF CITY TRUSTS.

PRESIDENTS OF THE BOARD OF DIRECTORS OF CITY TRUSTS.

WILLIAM WELSH
HENRY M. PHILLIPS
ALEXANDER BIDDLE

W. HEYWARD DRAYTON
LOUIS WAGNER

MEMBERS OF THE ORIGINAL BOARD OF DIRECTORS OF CITY TRUSTS, APPOINTED SEPTEMBER 2, 1869.

GUSTAVUS S. BENSON . . . . Died March 22, 1883.
ALEXANDER BIDDLE . . . . Resigned Jan. 12, 1885.
JAMES CAMPBELL . . . . Died Jan. 27, 1893.
JAMES L. CLAGHORN . . . . Died Aug. 25, 1884.
CHARLES H. T. COLLIS . . . . Resigned June 11, 1884.
J. GILLINGHAM FELL . . . . Resigned Sept. 9, 1874.
EDWARD KING . . . . Resigned Feb. 14, 1872.
WILLIAM B. MANN . . . . Died Oct. 17, 1896.
JOHN H. MICHENER . . . .
HENRY M. PHILLIPS . . . . Died Aug. 28, 1884.
GEORGE H. STUART . . . . Died April 11, 1890.
WILLIAM WELSH . . . . Died Feb. 11, 1878.

"EX-OFFICIO" MEMBERS.

DANIEL M. FOX, *Mayor* . . . . Term expired Jan. 1, 1872.
SAMUEL W. CATTELL, *President Select Council* . . Term expired Jan. 1, 1872.
LOUIS WAGNER, *President Common Council* . . . . Term expired Jan. 2, 1871.

APPOINTMENTS ON BOARD OF DIRECTORS OF CITY TRUSTS
SUBSEQUENT TO SEPTEMBER 2, 1869.

	Appointed.	
W. HEYWARD DRAYTON	Feb. 14, 1872.	Died Oct. 9, 1892.
LOUIS WAGNER	Jan. 4, 1875.	
GEORGE L. HARRISON	March 18, 1878.	Resigned Dec. 17, 1881.
BENJAMIN B. COMEGYS	Jan. 7, 1882.	
JOSEPH L. CAVEN	March 31, 1883.	
WILLIAM L. ELKINS	Oct. 6, 1884.	
JAMES SIMPSON, M.D.	Oct. 6, 1884.	Resigned March 5, 1888.
RICHARD VAUX	Oct. 6, 1884.	Died March 22, 1895.
WILLIAM HENRY RAWLE	Jan. 12, 1885.	Died April 19, 1889.
ALEXANDER BIDDLE (reappointed)	April 2, 1888.	
JOHN H. CONVERSE	June 3, 1889.	
EDWARD S. BUCKLEY	June 2, 1890.	
JOHN K. CUMING	Dec. 5, 1892.	
DALLAS SANDERS	March 6, 1893.	
JOHN MARIE CAMPBELL	April 15, 1895.	
EDWIN S. STUART	Dec. 7, 1896.	

"EX-OFFICIO" MEMBERS.

MAYORS.

WILLIAM S. STOKLEY	Jan. 1, 1872,	to April 4, 1881.
SAMUEL G. KING	April 4, 1881,	to April 7, 1884.
WILLIAM B. SMITH	April 7, 1884,	to April 4, 1887.
EDWIN H. FITLER	April 4, 1887,	to April 6, 1891.
EDWIN S. STUART	April 6, 1891,	to April 1, 1895.
CHARLES F. WARWICK	April 1, 1895.	

PRESIDENTS OF SELECT COUNCIL.

WM. E. LITTLETON	Jan. 1, 1872,	to Jan. 5, 1874.
* ROBERT W. DOWNING	Jan. 5, 1874,	to July 8, 1875.
W. W. BURNELL, M.D.	July 8, 1875,	to Jan. 3, 1876.
* GEORGE A. SMITH	Jan. 3, 1876,	to Nov. 3, 1881.
GEORGE W. BUMM	Nov. 3, 1881,	to April 3, 1882.
WILLIAM B. SMITH	April 3, 1882,	to April 7, 1884.
JAMES R. GATES	April 7, 1884,	to April 3, 1893.
JAMES L. MILES	April 3, 1893.	

* Resigned.

II

* HENRY HUHN . . . . Jan.	2, 1871, to Feb. 15, 1872.
LOUIS WAGNER . . . . Feb.	15, 1872, to Jan. 6, 1873.
A. W. HENSZEY . . . . Jan.	6, 1873, to Jan. 3, 1876.
JOSEPH L. CAVEN . . . . Jan.	3, 1876, to April 4, 1881.
WILLIAM H. LEX . . . . April	4, 1881, to April 7, 1884.
CHARLES LAWRENCE . . . . April	7, 1884, to April 2, 1888.
† WILLIAM M. SMITH . . . . April	2, 1888, to May 4, 1892.
WENCEL HARTMAN . . . . May	12, 1892.

The total number of Directors has been ninety-eight, but ten of these were elected to more than one term not consecutive; the longest term of service has been nineteen years, the shortest term, one year, and the average term, four years.

The total number of Directors of the City Trusts, not including members *ex officio*, has been twenty-eight; the longest term of service has been twenty-eight years, the shortest term, two years, and the average term, twelve years.

Mr. John H. Michener is the only member of the Board of Directors of City Trusts appointed on September 2, 1869, who has served continuously since that time.

Colonel Alexander Biddle resigned in January 12, 1885, and was reappointed April 2, 1888.

General Louis Wagner, who, as President of Common Council of the city of Philadelphia, was *ex officio* a member of the Board from 1869 to 1873, had also served from 1867 to 1869 as a member of Councils Committee on the Girard Estates.

Mr. Joseph L. Caven and Mr. Edwin S. Stuart had been *ex officio* members of the Board, as President of Common Council and as Mayor of the city of Philadelphia respectively, before their appointment as permanent members.

---

* Resigned.   † Died.

GIRARD COLLEGE: ITS ENDOWMENT AND MAINTENANCE, 1831–1898

BY GEORGE E. KIRKPATRICK,

Superintendent, Girard Estate.

When, on December 26, 1831, Stephen Girard died, he was said to be the wealthiest man in America. His estate, consisting largely of realty, much of it unimproved and undeveloped, was difficult to value. In a pamphlet published shortly after his death by direction of the Councils of the city of Philadelphia, it was estimated at from twelve to fifteen millions of dollars; but it was probably worth between five and seven millions.

In compliance with the directions given in the will, $96,000 was distributed in private charities; $140,000 and certain real estate in France were given to the relatives of Mr. Girard, and a number of bequests were paid to his employés. Certain interests and remainders in real and personal property located near Washita, in the State of Louisiana, were willed to the city of New Orleans for public improvements. The Commonwealth of Pennsylvania received $300,000, to be expended in internal improvements, and the remainder of his estate was devised to the city of Philadelphia in trust for the following charitable uses:

For school purposes in the first School District of Pennsylvania .	$10,000 00
For the distribution of fuel among the poor of the City of Philadelphia	10,000 00
For the improvement of the Eastern Front of the City of Philadelphia	500,000 00
For the erection of the Girard College Buildings, the necessary land worth probably	10,000 00
and a sum of	2,000,000 00
For the maintenance of the Girard College, the entire residue of the Estate, probably then worth	3,250,000 00
	$5,780,000 00

On April 20, 1833, the following securities were set aside as the fund for the erection of the Girard College buildings:

Stock of the Bank of the United States, 6,331 shares, valued at .	$664,715 00
Five per cent. Loan of the Commonwealth of Pennsylvania, $1,069,305, valued at	1,221,785 00
Five per cent. Loan of the City of Philadelphia, $100,000, valued at	113,500 00
Total	$2,000,000 00

At this time the stock of the Bank of the United States was paying a dividend of seven per cent. per annum, and both the Commonwealth of Pennsylvania and the city of Philadelphia were promptly paying the interest on their bonds; and it was hoped that, as considerable time would be required to erect the buildings, the income received from these securities would be sufficient to pay a large portion of the cost of erection, leaving a correspondingly large portion of the principal remain to increase the endowment fund.

The plan of the buildings designed by Mr. Thomas U. Walter, the architect, was adopted by the Councils of the city of Philadelphia on April 29, 1833. Work was begun on May 6, 1833, and the corner-stone of the Main Building was laid on July 4 of the same year. The work progressed favorably until 1839, when the income of the building fund was greatly reduced by the financial panic and disaster which had swept over the country. The Bank of the United States had failed. Interest on the bonds of the Commonwealth of Pennsylvania was paid in six per cent. bonds, which sold for less than fifty cents on the dollar, or later in " relief notes," which also sold at a heavy discount. The fund for the erection of the College buildings suffered greatly from these causes. The income, out of which it was expected to pay for the erection, was cut off or reduced to a comparatively small sum. To continue the work of erection, it was necessary either to sell a portion of the principal of the fund or to greatly reduce the extent of the work undertaken.

Under the financial conditions then prevailing, the former course would involve serious sacrifice, which it was hoped could be avoided by curtailing the work until the business depression should pass, and from 1840 to 1844 the erection of the buildings made slow progress.

This course, however, did not prevent the sacrifice of the invested funds, all of which had to be sold at such prices as could be obtained, and the buildings could only be completed by encroaching upon the Residuary Fund.

The cash realized from the $2,000,000 building fund amounted to:

Sale of Investments, originally valued at $2,000,000		$1,099,186 70
Interest and Dividends collected		851,146 98
		$1,950,333 68
The cost of the Buildings was	$1,933,821 78	
and the collateral expenses	49,624 21	
		1,983,445 99
Excess of expense		$33,112 31

This excess of expense was made up by

Sales of Waste Materials	$1,587 20
and an appropriation from the Residuary Fund of	31,525 11
	$33,112 31

After the payment of all the specific bequests, including with these the amounts willed for the erection of the College buildings and for the improvement of the eastern front of the city, etc., there remained the main portion of Mr. Girard's real estate, consisting of the banking house on Third Street, a number of stores, warehouses, dwellings, wharves and vacant lots in the city of Philadelphia; a number of dwellings and over six hundred acres of farm land and lots in Philadelphia County; seventy-three tracts of land "on the Mahanoy" (Schuylkill and Columbia Counties, Pennsylvania) containing over twenty-nine thousand acres; six thousand acres of land in Erie County, Pennsylvania; four thousand seven hundred and seventy-five acres in Hart County, Kentucky; two undivided third parts of a tract of land in Louisiana, containing two hundred and seven thousand acres, and stocks and bonds with an aggregate par value of $488,104.13.

This remainder (called the Residuary Fund) was devoted by Mr. Girard's will, first to the maintenance and extension of Girard College, within the limits of the designated tract of land on Ridge Road, known as the Peel Hall farm; and, second, for city purposes, the support of a police force, to improve city property and the general appearance of the city, and to diminish the burden of taxation.

Much of this property was lost to the fund. The real estate acquired after the last republication of the will was recovered by Mr. Girard's heirs-at-law. This included a number of tracts in Schuylkill County, some of which have since proven to be very valuable coal land. The land in Erie County and in Louisiana was lost through defective titles. An error was discovered in the survey of the land described in the Kentucky deeds, and a large portion of this property was thus found to have no existence; while the value of the stocks and bonds was in time found to be less than one-half of their face.

The income from the Residuary Fund, by the terms of the will devoted primarily to the support of the College, could not be so applied until the buildings were completed. Because of this, the Councils of the city of Philadelphia determined that, pending the completion of the buildings, this income should be applied toward its secondary object, viz., city purposes; the support of a police force, improvement of city property and the lightening of the burden of taxation. In this manner, $571,958.42 was expended as follows:

Stores, Wharf, Dock, etc., near the Schuylkill River	$18,000 00
Railroad on Broad Street	6,028 55
Culvert at Drawbridge Dock	4,000 00
Paving and Repairing Streets	64,971 45
Rebuilding Market-Houses on High Street	20,000 00
Iron Mains for the Distribution of Water	23,000 00
Tobacco Warehouse	7,000 00
Improvements at Fairmount	28,000 00
Lamp-Posts, Lamps, etc.	20,950 00
Improvements of Public Squares	11,000 00
Repairing Wharves	3,750 00
Culverts	8,300 00
General City Purposes, Police, etc. (not specified)	303,208 42
Diminishing Taxation and Supplying Deficiencies	53,750 00
	$571,958 42

Upon the completion of the College buildings and the opening of the Institution on January 1, 1848, these expenditures for city purposes ceased, and since that time the entire net income of the Residuary Fund has been applied toward the support and maintenance of the Girard College.

In spite of all its losses and depreciations, the Residuary Fund has increased until to-day it may safely be valued at over twenty million dollars, exclusive of the Girard College grounds and buildings. When this fund was received by the city, its income amounted to between sixty and seventy thousand dollars per annum. In 1848, this had increased to one hundred and eighteen thousand dollars per annum,—a sum ample, after deducting the expenses of the Estate, to support the Institution with the number of pupils then contemplated,—300. Up to this time, the growth in income was due entirely to real estate in the vicinity of Philadelphia, which in 1848 yielded $109,742.38. As this property has become more valuable and as buildings have been erected upon the vacant lots, or new buildings have taken the place of the old structures which changing conditions had made unprofitable, the revenue derived therefrom has continued to increase, in 1897 being $415,044.18.

The most important of these building improvements were:

1858-9.   12 Dwellings on the north side of Brown Street, between Fifth and Sixth Streets.
1871-4.   43 Dwellings on Fifth, Sixth and Marshall Streets between Fairmount Avenue and Brown, and on the south side of Brown Street between Fifth and Sixth Streets.
1874.   The Banking House and Office Building, 433-437 Chestnut Street.

1886-7. The store on the southwest corner of Eleventh and Market Streets (Nos. 1100–1114).

1887-9. The row of stores between the above and Twelfth Street (Nos. 1120–1142).

1896-7. The Stephen Girard Building, 19–25 South Twelfth Street.

Plans for the erection of the twenty-two stores and fifty-six dwellings upon the block between Eleventh and Twelfth, Market and Chestnut Streets, were under consideration by Mr. Girard for some time before his death; the actual improvement was made after his death by his executors, and not by the city as trustee.

The income from Real Estate in Schuylkill and Columbia Counties amounted to little prior to 1863; but in that year the mining of coal upon this property began, the gross receipts being $3,770.87. These receipts have increased from year to year, as new collieries have been opened or facilities for mining improved, and in 1897 amounted to $532,855.76.

The radical difference between royalty upon coal mined and removed from the property, and rental where the property is returned at the end of the lease "in like good order and condition" does not seem to have been taken into consideration in the early days of mining on the property of the Girard Estate; but in 1877 the fact that the mining of coal is a depletion of the realty, was recognized by the inauguration of a policy under which three-fourths of the net income derived from this source has been treated as principal and set aside for investment. Early in 1897, this policy was extended, the entire net income being now treated as capital.

The amount of the cash receipts thus set aside for investment, to December 31, 1897, is $7,028,077.72, and from this source have been derived the funds with which to make the recent extensive improvements to real estate within the city, and to increase the value of the investments in stocks and loans from $300,000, in 1862, to $4,750,000 on December 31, 1897, and the annual income derived therefrom, from $8,288.40 to $230,516.25.

By his will, Mr. Girard charged upon his real estate in the Commonwealth of Pennsylvania a number of annuities aggregating $3,900 per annum. The payment of these continued until 1896, when the last annuitant died, and the amount thus expended was $89,550.00.

With steadily increasing income available for its support, the Girard College has been enlarged, in the number of its buildings, from five to nineteen, and in their value from $2,000,000 to $3,300,000; while the number of pupils has increased from 300 to 1550.

This enlargement began in 1850, when Building No. 5 was erected.

The other more important improvements in buildings and in the equipment of the College were as follows:

1858.	Infirmary Building (No. 6).
1876–77.	Building No. 7.
1876–77.	Chapel.
1876–77.	East Boiler House, Bakery, Laundry.
1877–78.	Heating by steam from a central plant.
1880–81.	Building No. 8.
1880–81.	First Extension of Infirmary Building.
1883–84.	West Boiler House.
1883–84.	Mechanical School Building.
1885–86.	Building No. 9.
1887.	Exterior Electric Lighting.
1887–89.	Greenhouse.
1889–90.	Building No. 10.
1889–90.	New Laundry and Bakery.
1894.	Interior Electric Lighting.
1897.	Second Extension of Infirmary Building.

Summing the financial transactions of the Girard College, and of the Residuary Fund, from the death of Mr. Girard until December 31, 1897, a period of sixty-six years (during the last fifty of which the College has cared for and educated nearly 6,000 orphan boys), we have in round figures:

Value in 1831–35 of the Girard College and Residuary Funds :

Real Estate, Philadelphia City and County . .	$1,500,000	
Buildings erected at Twelfth and Market Streets by the Executors	750,000	
		$2,250,000 00
Girard College Grounds		10,000 00
Real Estate outside of Philadelphia		500,000 00
Stocks and Bonds		2,500,000 00
		$5,260,000 00

Increase in the value of the above property (1831–1898) :

Real Estate, Philadelphia	$2,550,000	
Girard College Grounds	1,690,000	
Real Estate outside of Philadelphia		
Converted into cash and invested $7,000,000		
Unconverted 7,500,000	14,500,000	
		18,740,000 00

Net income collected :

Real Estate, Philadelphia	$9,125,000	
Real Estate outside of Philadelphia (exclusive of amount capitalized)	3,200,000	
Stocks and Bonds	3,700,000	
Miscellaneous Sources	162,000	
		16,187,000 00
		$40,187,000 00
Decrease in value of Stocks and Bonds . . .		1,250,000 00
		$38,937,000 00

From which there has been expended for

Annuities	$90,000	
City Purposes	572,000	
Girard College (maintenance)	11,350,000	
		$12,012,000 00
And there remains on December 31, 1897 . .		$26,925,000 00

Consisting of

Girard College Grounds . . .	$1,700,000		
" " . Buildings . . .	3,300,000		
		$5,000,000	
Real Estate in Philadelphia		9,000,000	
Real Estate outside of Philadelphia		8,000,000	
Stocks and Bonds		4,900,000	
Cash		25,000	
			$26,925,000 00

With this steady growth in invested principal and in income, it is safe to predict that there will be other additions to the buildings of the Girard College and further increase in the number of its pupils, until the capacity of the College grounds shall have been reached, and that thereafter large amounts of surplus revenue will be available "to diminish the burden of taxation" upon the citizens of Philadelphia.

GIRARD COLLEGE.   BATTALION OF CADETS, ON WEST PLAYGROUND.

GIRARD COLLEGE: ITS TRAINING AND THE RESULTS

BY JOHN S. BOYD, M.D.,

Superintendent of Admission and Indentures.

To ascertain the results of the magnificent endowment of Girard College, we need only to call attention to the number of pupils who, within its walls, have shared in the training, and to speak of their present success, by which they show what this training has produced.

First, as to the condition of many of these pupils when they enter: They are between the ages of six and ten; some of them commencing without the simplest rudiments of education, and none of them having progressed beyond what can be obtained in the lower grades of elementary schools.

During six or more years, of systematic and thorough instruction, they have been advanced from class to class, attention being paid at all times to their physical health; and they have received a careful training of the mind and heart. The transformation is complete, and they go forth prepared to meet the requirements of the world possessors of "mens sana in corpore sano."

What becomes of the graduates of Girard College?

It needed for an answer but an opportunity to gaze at the platoons of well-dressed and intelligent young men, all graduates of Girard College, marching in military array past the City Hall on the occasion of the unveiling on May 20, 1897, of the bronze statue of their benefactor.

To answer this question in an official manner, it was decided by the Board of Directors of City Trusts and the Alumni to collect statistics concerning the graduates now living. With this purpose in view, the Alumni appointed a special committee of twenty-eight, with Mr. Thomas Orr as Chairman, and Mr. Frederick Unrath as Secretary (and to Mr. Unrath much of the credit for the completeness of their report is due).

In reply to their inquiries, the following results have been obtained:

Admitted since the opening of the College		5899
Died in the College		174
		5725
Number enrolled December 31, 1897		1536
Discharged, and to be accounted for		4189
Number reported as employed	2073	
Number reported as unemployed	191	
Died since leaving College	380	
Readmitted	5	
In other institutions	17	
No report	1523	
		4189

As has already been stated in the *Public Ledger*, the pupils enter the College "at a tender age and are discharged at the age of eighteen, so that it is impossible to do anything more than prepare them for a college education, or for work; and as the greater number of graduates are dependent upon themselves for support, few of them obtain any other education than that given within the College walls. Under these circumstances, it is not to be expected that the roll of Alumni should exhibit the names of men of letters, such as may be found in the list of graduates of universities; but it is largely to the credit of the Institution that, substantially, all the graduates have become good citizens. Some among the number have risen to high position in the professions, using the elementary education at the College as the foundation for private studies. There is no doubt that the education is thorough so far as it goes, and that, considering the age of the pupils, Girard College deserves to rank among the best of elementary schools."

When boys leave school, they are, of necessity, lacking in the ease of manner and the knowledge of that technical language which can only be acquired from actual association with men and women in the busy, practical world about them; and it is gratifying, if not surprising, to note the rapidity with which Girard College boys attain that polish of address and familiarity with the variety of details which render them distinguishable from the average young men of business with whom they daily come in contact. They take pride, furthermore, in their personal appearance and their moral reputation, are ambitious to advance in the positions they occupy; and with reference to the impression which is probably, even at this day, extensively prevalent, not only in this city but elsewhere, in regard to the neglect of religious training in Girard College, the best answer that we can make is, that very many of our graduates manifest a most commendable interest and zeal in religious affairs. They are also disposed to establish quite early in their career homes of their own, and are evidently deeply attached to the families that surround their hearthstones.

Since the reports which have been received from former pupils are, in the majority of instances, from those who have been more recently graduated, it is but reasonable to assume that the proportion, in a complete list, of those occupying prominent positions in professional and business life is even greater than as now presented.

Examining in detail the long list of occupations (more than three hundred in number) in which these graduates are engaged, we find that, in the professions, those who have been admitted to the bar are highest in number, eighteen, while four are enrolled as students having the same purpose in view; ten are clergymen and two more are students; ten are physicians and surgeons and four are students; there are two dentists and one student; there are seven druggists, twelve drug clerks, and three chemists; three are civil engineers, one is a student and one is a surveyor; five are architects and one is studying in the same branch of art; eleven are draughtsmen and four are contractors; there are four notaries public, two of whom are conveyancers; five are teachers, five prefects, and twenty are students. In banking and kindred pursuits there are two bankers and brokers, three assistant cashiers of banks, two bank tellers; five treasurers and four with the title of secretary and treasurer, and eighteen are connected with the insurance business. The list of bank and railroad clerks is very large, but they are embraced in a general class as clerks or bookkeepers, which reaches the large total of four hundred and eighty. There are seventy-seven stenographers, eighty salesmen, two paymasters, and six cashiers. Five are auditors, twelve are in the real estate business, ten are superintendents or assistant superintendents, fifteen are inspectors and thirty-three are managers in various industries. Mining and railroads have their representatives, nine are journalists, two publishers, and two reporters; and in the public service fifteen are letter-carriers and ten policemen, and nineteen are railway conductors.

In other spheres of usefulness we find some who are merchants and dealers, some manufacturers, twenty-five foremen of various kinds, fifty-six printers and four proofreaders; twenty-four are plumbers, either employers or journeymen; twenty-seven carpenters and four pattern-makers; twenty electricians, seventeen engineers, thirteen engravers, sixty-five machinists, three tool-makers, thirteen moulders, eleven tinsmiths, ten hatters, ten miners, thirty paper-hangers (nine of whom are employers), twenty-nine painters (six being employers), seventy factory hands, and fifty-three farmers. Sixteen are cutters, twelve blacksmiths, four designers, and one is a sculptor; five are florists or gardeners, nineteen are packers and shippers, eleven upholsterers, thirteen weavers, six undertakers and embalmers, and fifteen are engaged in the baking or confectionery business.

Four are now students in the Williamson Free School of Mechanical Trades; six are in the United States Navy, three are seamen, and two are in the United States Army (one of whom is a lieutenant); and one is a Commissioner of Immigration, one a Deputy Collector of Customs, one a Deputy Recorder of Deeds, and one is a tipstaff.

Appended to the above report is a schedule showing the nativity of parents of boys admitted to the College from January 1, 1870, to December 31, 1897,—4521 in number:

12

	Father.	Mother.
United States	2891	3109
Ireland	576	565
Germany	549	424
England	283	222
Wales	63	68
Scotland	47	62
France	27	22
Switzerland	14	9
Canada	11	8
Cuba	8	3
Italy	8	2
Sweden	6	3
Nova Scotia	5	2
Russia	5	2
Norway	5	2
Holland	5	1
Denmark	3	1
Austria	3	2
Palestine	2	2
Portugal	2	0
South America	1	1
Mexico	0	2
West Indies	0	1
Newfoundland	0	1
Belgium	1	0
East Indies	0	1
Australia	0	1
On shipboard	0	1
Not recorded	6	4
	4521	4521

www.ingramcontent.com/pod-product-compliance
Lightning Source LLC
Chambersburg PA
CBHW031954060726
47497CB00016B/2143